'I can't explain that, Gemma,

I just know there's been something...' Palms up, Sam spread his long, narrow hands eloquently. 'Something since day one... I'm sorry. Have I embarrassed you, scared you?'

Gemma tried to clear her throat. 'You didn't scare me or embarrass me,' then, firmly, in her normal voice, she added, 'No, not at all, but...'

'But...what do we do about it?'

CHAPTER ONE

THE waiting room was nearly full and every other person seemed to be coughing and sneezing. There was no one behind the reception desk.

Gemma waited patiently, reminding herself that this was a small village surgery, buried in the heart of rural Dorset. She musn't expect the same fast tempo she had been used to in the busy, high-tech town practice she had left behind her.

'You might have a long wait, love,' one of the coughers and sneezers spluttered out, his voice not only thick with cold but with the local burr. 'Dr Sam's on his own—the old doctor's out on an emergency, Ellie's off sick, and Mrs Mallory can't get here for a bit.'

This mine of information was an elderly man, sitting in one of the front chairs in the waiting area. He smiled cheerfully at Gemma when she turned round.

She smiled back. 'Any idea how long that is likely to be?'

'You can ask the doctor now,' said the elderly man, nodding towards the archway that opened off the waiting room.

A tall, fair-haired man stood in the archway, his head and shoulders bent down towards the diminutive little old lady standing beside him. She was wearing a deaf aid. He said in a loud voice, laying a hand on her tiny shoulder, 'Come back in a day or two, Mrs Bryce, if the tablets don't work. Or if you can't make it to the surgery, give us a buzz and we'll come to you.'

Well, now I know I'm in never, never land, thought Gemma, a doctor who actually *offers* to visit.

The old lady beamed up at him. 'I won't do that unless I have to, Doctor. You know me, like to keep toddling round, stops me old joints from seizing up.' And thumping her stick, she made her shaky way along the short corridor towards the exit.

Gemma nipped in front of her and held open the door. The old lady nodded. 'Thank you, dear.'

The doctor crossed the waiting room and slid behind the reception desk. He pulled a book crammed with names towards him and smiled at Gemma. 'Have you—' The phone rang. He shrugged. 'Sorry.' Then he picked up the receiver. 'Surgery... Right, Pam, keep her warm, give her lots to drink—somebody will be over to see her as soon as possible.'

He added a few squiggles to a memo pad beside the phone, then looked across at Gemma. 'Sorry about that. Now, how can I help you? Have you an appointment?'

He had a nice voice, a rich tenor, tinged with the faintest of Dorset accents. Fringed by thick, silky brown lashes, vivid blue eyes enhanced by the blue of an open-necked shirt—intelligent, enquiring—surveyed her over the desk.

'I've come to register myself and my daughter with your practice—we've just moved into the village—but you're so busy, perhaps...'

He gave her a wide smile. His eyes smiled, too. 'If you *could* come back later, you'd be doing me a favour—we're a bit short-handed this morning.'

'So I gather... Look, could I be of any help?' The suggestion came out in a rush, surprising herself as much as it obviously surprised the doctor, whose eyebrows shot up. 'I'm a registered general nurse with practice experience and have done the odd stint as receptionist.'

Instantly, his manner changed, grew distant. 'Thanks for the kind offer, but I'm afraid I can't take you up on it. You're a stranger, and I can't simply take your word for it that you're fully qualified, Ms…' He sounded faintly apologetic.

'Mrs Fellows,' she said briskly. Her cheeks reddened, her emerald green eyes blazed. 'Of course you can't—it was a silly suggestion. I may be a drug addict or a Nosy Parker wanting a peek at medical files. I'll let you get on, Doctor, and come back later to register.'

You prat, she said to herself as, stiff-backed, she marched down the corridor towards the exit. Fancy making such a fool of yourself and putting the poor man on the spot like that. You and your big mouth.

Sam Mallory stared at her rigid back, her smooth, neat bob of shining reddish brown hair swinging from side to side and at her neatly trousered rounded buttocks. Her back view, he thought, definitely looked cross—more than cross. It radiated fury, with him and with herself he guessed. And her eyes had blazed fury a moment before. *Honest* fury. He whisked round the desk and in a few long strides caught up with her.

He stopped her at the door. 'That was a stupid attitude for me to take,' he said in a low voice. 'It's pretty obvious that you've nothing to hide, but one has to be so careful these days, even in a village like Blaney St Mary.'

Gemma took a deep breath. 'Of course you do,' she said. 'Don't worry about it. Message received and understood. I'll come back this afternoon to sign on.'

'No!' He touched her arm. His touch was light, but she could feel the pressure of his fingertips through her jacket. Her arm tingled. 'Look, can you lay your hands on your registration certificate?'

'Of course I can, and my CV and references—why?' Her precious documents had been the first things she'd unpacked and filed safely away.

'Will you fetch them? If you're in the village you can't be far.'

Gemma frowned. 'I'm just across the green, but—'

'Please,' he begged, his eyes serious. 'We could do with some help. At present we're without a nurse *or* a receptionist. You're God's gift, manna from heaven, as they say.' He grinned. 'Please, give me a chance to make amends for giving you such a hasty brush-off.'

She swallowed a knot of excitement and surprise that rose in her throat. 'Are you offering me a job, or do you just want help today?'

The phone rang. He took a step backwards and shrugged, then ran a hand through his thick thatch of corn-fair hair. 'Either, whatever... Look, I must answer that. Come back with the necessary and we'll talk—say in about three quarters of an hour. I'll be through with most of my patients by then and my father will be back from his rounds.'

Feeling as if she were walking on air, Gemma floated across the green to Cherry Tree Cottage. The cottage was one of a small terrace facing the wide expanse of grass fringed with trees. She knew she wasn't dreaming, but her conversation with the doctor had a dreamlike quality about it. It looked as if by chance, luck or fate, in one fell swoop she had solved her greatest problem—she was going to land herself a much-needed job. It could, she felt, only have happened in an off-the-map place like Blaney St Mary.

Having to leave London and her job, that had been the only flaw that had presented itself when she had learned that her great-aunt Marjorie, with whom she had corresponded only at Christmas, had bequeathed her the cottage. But it was a small price to pay for the privilege of owning her own mortgage-free house, rather than a cramped flat. A house to make into a home for herself and Daisy, a real home.

She glanced up the long oval green towards the village school, and prayed that Daisy was settling into her new environment. It was a dramatic change from the large primary school she had been attending. Not that Daisy had had any qualms—she had seemed quite happy when Gemma had left her earlier in the care of the young, breezy headmistress, Joy Scott. But, then, she was a happy little girl. It had been Gemma who'd been nervous.

In reversal of the mother-daughter roles, Daisy had squeezed Gemma's hand with her small, pudgy one, and said firmly, 'I'll be all right, Mummy. I know I'm going to like it here, it's pretty, like a doll's-size school.'

Compared to her old school, a shabby edifice of concrete and glass, it *was* pretty and doll-sized. It was a bungalow-type building, all red tiles and rose bricks, tucked away just off the green amongst trees and flowerbeds and surrounded by a large play area.

Gemma had squeezed her hand in return. 'I'm sure you're going to be fine, love.' She had dropped a kiss on her daughter's soft, round cheek and had smoothed back a tendril of reddish brown hair. 'I'll be here to collect you at three o'clock. Don't go anywhere until I come.'

Miss Scott had said, calmly reassuring, 'Don't worry, Mrs Fellows, there's always someone here to see every child safely off the premises.'

Assured that Daisy was safe till three o'clock, Gemma let herself through the tiny flower-filled front garden into the cottage, ducking beneath the branches of the ancient cherry tree that gave it its name.

Picking her way round the boxes still waiting to be unpacked, she made for the bureau in the sitting room, where she had filed all her important documents. Her registration certificate, CV and references were among them.

Glancing at the glowing reference from Jonathan Willet, head of the busy Nine Elms practice she had worked for until a few weeks ago, she experienced a moment's nostalgia.

It was a fleeting moment gone in a flash, but it triggered off memories and she wallowed a bit as she sat at the kitchen table, nursing a mug of coffee. She had no real regrets about leaving London. She had a few close friends, and they would keep in touch, perhaps visit occasionally. But there was no one she would miss desperately. She and Daisy had always been rather on their own.

A lone parent with a small baby, she'd discovered soon after she and Neil had split up, had little time, money or energy to spare for socialising. Her girl friends and a couple of male friends, doctors and nurses from her training days, were either absorbed in stable relationships or making the most of being completely fancy-free agents. They visited sometimes, and she, with baby Daisy, had visited them—that had been the extent of her social life for the last few years.

Remembering, it brought the sting of tears to the back of her eyes. That was when she could have done with loving parents to support her, she thought sadly. If only Mum and Dad hadn't parted in a messy divorce, weren't living on opposite sides of the world with new partners... *Stop that!* she told herself savagely. Stop getting maudlin. Things are looking up, so don't start feeling sorry for yourself.

Mentally, she totted up her blessings. We're living in a lovely house in a pretty village, and Daisy's school is brilliant—and to top it all, you've *almost* been handed a job on a platter. And it could be a plum of a job in a great set-up with doctors who obviously cared, and all within a stone's throw of home and school.

Two coffees and half an hour later, her heart beating unevenly in anticipation of her interview with Dr Mallory junior—Dr Sam, as the locals called him—Gemma made her way back across the green to the surgery.

The waiting room was empty of patients, but a tall, thin man with a thatch of dark blonde hair, silvered at the temples, was unloading buff record envelopes from a briefcase behind the reception desk. He looked up as Gemma entered. There was no mistaking the blue eyes, the corn-coloured hair. He had to be 'the old doctor'—Dr Mallory senior.

Smiling his son's wide, generous smile in a similarly lean face, he said, 'It's Mrs Fellows, isn't it?'

Gemma, suppressing a surprised intake of breath, returned his smile. 'Yes—but how on earth do you know who I am?'

He raised thick, straight eyebrows. 'You're a stranger—we don't get many of those in the village except in high summer. And the second clue—my son told me to expect you about now, and for good measure gave me a sort of thumbnail description which fits you perfectly.' His eyes twinkled and Gemma wondered just how the younger doctor had portrayed her.

A frisson of pleasure rippled through her at the thought that he had noticed her enough to describe her accurately.

'Oh,' she said lamely. 'I didn't realise that strangers were in quite such short supply. I must stick out like a sore thumb.'

Dr Mallory gave a little snort of laughter, his eyes glinting with admiration. 'Anything but a sore thumb, my dear, I assure you.' He finished unloading the patients' records from his briefcase and joined Gemma on the other side of the desk. 'Now, Mrs Fellows, what about you and I going through to my office and having a chat while we wait for Sam? Get to know each other a little. He'll join us shortly—his last patient is with him now.'

His office looked out over a large, walled garden at the rear of the single-storey surgery block. A mossy, gabled roof and ancient twisted chimneys were visible between the tops of trees, above a froth of pink and white blossom. There was a tall gate in the flint wall opposite the window.

'Oh how lovely,' Gemma exclaimed.

The doctor waved a hand toward the window. 'Our orchard—apples, pears and plums mostly. Blossoming spectacularly early this year, due to an extremely mild winter. We don't exactly live over the shop, but next door to it. That's Timbers you can see above the trees. I was born there and so were all our children. Can't imagine living anywhere else, though it's too big for us nowadays, even though Sam has his own self-contained wing. My wife and I rattle around in it, except when our brood descends upon us *en masse*.'

His voice had a warm ring to it, making no bones of his pride in his home and family.

So Dr Sam lived in the family home. Surprising for a man in what—his mid-thirties? But why not? It made sense in a house of that size, and was convenient for the surgery. And his 'wing' is probably several times bigger than Cherry Tree Cottage—enough to house his own brood of corn-blonde children?

Gemma pulled her wayward thoughts up sharply. Whatever had sent them off on such a tangent? The doctor's domestic arrangements were his own affair, and certainly nothing to do with her.

'Have you got a large family, Dr Mallory?' she asked.

'Another son and two daughters, all married, all with offspring.' He grinned. 'But I musn't bore you with family talk—bad as looking at people's holiday snaps. Now, please, do sit down and tell me about yourself. I've only had a brief chat with my son, but I understand you're a qualified nurse. Where did you train, Mrs Fellows?'

She breathed an inward sigh of relief. This was better...this she could handle.

'City Central, but for the last three years I've been working in a London health centre as a practice nurse. I have a current reference from the head of the practice, Dr Willet.' She fished that and her CV out of her bag.

'Jonathan Willet, about my age, a Barts man?'

'Yes.'

The doctor grinned. 'We trained together, met up once or twice on courses since—nice chap.' He held out his hand. 'So, what's my old friend got to say about you, Mrs Fellows?'

Gemma handed him the wallet of papers and blushed. 'He's been very generous about my work.'

'Well deserved, I'm sure.' He put on a pair of rimless half-specs and had just finished reading the reference when there was a tap on the door. 'That'll be Sam. Come in,' he called. He smiled at Gemma. 'This is going to please him. Here, Sam, read this. It's from Jonathan Willet, that's who Mrs Fellows was working for.' He thrust the letter of reference into his son's hands.

The younger doctor gave her a fleeting smile as he took the document from his father. His eyes, she realised, were a more vivid blue than the older man's, and he was a little taller—six feet three or four, she guessed.

He skimmed through the closely worded page and his lean face creased into a wider smile. 'I'm impressed,' he said softly. 'Obviously Dr Willet was sorry to lose you, and presumably you were happy there, so may I ask what made you move to Blaney St Mary, Mrs Fellows?'

'I inherited a house here from my great-aunt, Mrs Rivers.'

'Of course—Cherry Tree Cottage!' said Dr Mallory senior. 'I should have realised. Not that Mrs Rivers spent much time in the cottage, but it's nice to know that it is to be occupied by someone with village connections.'

Sam Mallory laughed. 'Dad, you're coming over all patriarchal again.' He turned to Gemma and pulled a rueful face. 'My father hates change and we've lived in Blaney so long he feels personally responsible for everyone in and around the village.'

Gemma said impulsively. 'I think that's rather nice. Better than being somewhere where no one cares.'

'I'm glad someone appreciates me,' said the old doctor dryly, with a sly look at his son. Then he added formally. 'Welcome to Blaney St Mary, Mrs Fellows. Now to get down to business. I understand you have a daughter— but she can't be very old. Will your husband be able to cope with looking after her, should we offer you the post of practice nurse?'

'Daisy's six, and she started school here this morning. I'm divorced, so there isn't anyone to help care for her. I would only be able to work school hours initially, but perhaps more if I can find a registered reliable child-minder.' With a sinking heart, she looked anxiously from one doctor and to the other. 'Does that put me out of the running for the job?'

They both shook their heads. 'Not at all,' said Sam. 'My mother will always do some part-time nursing to cover out-of-school hours if needed.' He grinned. 'She's brilliant at spreading herself around—a sort of super-woman, my mother.'

Dr Mallory senior grinned in a similar fashion. 'That's for sure,' he said, his voice warm and affectionate. 'School holidays might be a bit of a problem, but we'll cross that bridge when we come to it. By then, both you and Daisy will have made some friends so child-minding may not be a difficulty.' He slanted his son a questioning look. 'So, what do you say, Sam? Shall we take Mrs Fellows on board?'

His voice was teasing. Clearly he'd made up his mind. Her connection with Jonathan Willet had been the clincher, Gemma guessed. What about his son? He had sounded encouraging but... For a second, Gemma found herself holding her breath.

Sam met Gemma's anxious eyes and said softly, reassuringly, 'With a reference like that, how can we refuse?' He held out his hand. Gemma slid hers into it. It felt strong, warm and comforting. 'Welcome to the practice, Gemma.'

Lying in bed that night, Gemma sleepily reviewed the events of the day. It had been a magical day, she thought, a day of small miracles. She had acquired a job and Daisy had loved her first day in her new school, having already acquired a—*best*—friend.

Sharp at three, a noisy crowd of excited children had poured out of school. Daisy had come racing over to where Gemma had stood waiting with several other mums and an occasional dad—hand in hand with another small girl.

Side by side, they had bounced up and down in front of Gemma. 'Mummy, this is Katy,' Daisy had announced breathlessly. 'She's my best friend. Miss Scott said she had to look after me, 'cos she sits next to me at our table.'

'Hello, Katy.' Gemma had smiled down at the skinny, fair-haired little girl with the bobbing plaits. 'Thank you for looking after Daisy. It's nice to have a friend when you start in a new school.'

Katy, suddenly solemn, had said, 'That's what *Miss* said, so I had to show Daisy where everything's kept in cupboards and places so she'll know tomorrow.'

'And now I know,' Daisy had said, with her particular brand of adult pragmatism. 'But we're still going to be best friends.'

'Yes,' Katy had replied, giving an extra big bounce, 'we are.'

A woman who turned out to be Katy's mother had arrived at that moment to claim her daughter. She had introduced herself as Mary Martin. 'I hope Katy hasn't been making a nuisance of herself,' she'd said to Gemma. 'She's an awful chatterbox.'

'Not at all,' Gemma had reassured her. 'She's been looking after Daisy, showing her the ropes, and I don't think anybody could out-chatterbox my daughter.'

'Wanna bet?' Mary Martin had laughed as she had steered Katy away, turning into the lane beside the school.

Gemma and Daisy made their way up the green to Cherry Tree Cottage, Daisy dancing ahead and babbling on about all that had happened at school. It was a typical early April day of scudding white puffs of cloud and high wind. Gemma, half running to keep up with Daisy, decided she would tell her daughter about her new job when they were having tea.

Half-asleep, recalling her daughter's response to the news, she smiled into the near darkness. Moonlight glimmered through the cotton curtains. It had been so typically Daisy. She had slid from her chair, trotted round the table, thrown her arms round Gemma's neck and given her a resounding kiss. 'Now,' she had said, sounding like a wise little old lady, 'there aren't *any* flies in the ointment, are there?' And Gemma had remembered having once referred to the lack of a job as being 'the only fly in the ointment' in regard to the move to Blaney St Mary.

'No flies at all,' she'd confirmed happily.

Gemma snuggled deeper into the duvet, on the edge of sleep, thinking of tomorrow and starting work at the surgery. She was sure she was going to enjoy working with the two Drs Mallory and all the indications were that Mrs Olivia Mallory—Sam's superwoman mother—was going to be fun to work with.

Not that Olivia Mallory had looked anything like the woman Gemma had expected from Sam's description. Like her husband and son she was fair-haired, but unlike them she was short and plump, a bustling little woman with kind hazel eyes.

When Dr Mallory had introduced her as 'Livy, my wife, who keeps us all in order', Gemma had thought he had been affectionately teasing. The idea that he or his son would be ordered about by anyone was a joke for, in spite of their friendliness, they both possessed an air of authority.

Yet within minutes of arriving in the surgery, Mrs Mallory had sent her husband off to his office to catch up with his paperwork and her son off on his house calls. When the men had gone, she said. 'Now, Gemma—you don't mind if I call you Gemma?' Gemma had shaken her head. 'I'll show you round and fill you in on the nursing and reception routine.'

She'd opened a door. 'This is...'

Gemma's eyelids closed as sleep overtook her.

On the other side of the green, Sam Mallory was trying to switch off after a hectically busy day. Thank God the regular locum they used was on call for the night.

He sat in his favourite leather armchair in his large, comfortable sitting room, nursing a glass of whisky and thinking about Gemma Fellows and the miracle that had brought her into the surgery that morning. She had been the shining spot in his otherwise overworked day, a day that had ended sadly in the death of an old patient.

His mind switched to Tom Bowles. OK, so Tom had been eighty, chronically bronchitic and had refused to be hospitalised when pneumonia had set in. Although well cared for by his devoted daughter, it had been almost inevitable that he should die as a result of this latest attack of pneumonia. But the fact that Tom had been old didn't stop Sam from mourning his death.

As a small boy, he had trotted round after old Tom when he had worked in the garden at Timbers. It had, he recalled with a smile, been

Tom who had taught him the value of earthworms in the scheme of things. And now he was dead.

Sam heaved a sigh and comforted himself with the thought that at least he'd got to his bedside before the end, and had been able to give the old boy an injection to ease the rattling, painful breathing.

He took a swig of whisky. The rosy firelight, glinting on the liquid in the glass, reminded him of Gemma's gleaming red-brown hair streaming out behind her as he had watched her racing across the green, chasing her daughter. There was no doubt that the little girl *was* her daughter—her bronzed red hair gave her away. He had spotted them as he was leaving a patient's house and had been captivated by the sight.

How, he wondered—as he emptied his glass, were the lovely Gemma and her pretty daughter going to fit into Blaney St Mary? It was a far cry from a noisy, crowded London suburb. Would they, and particularly Gemma, settle down? He was confident that little Daisy would—children were so adaptable—but her mother? Would she hanker after the bright lights, theatres, clubs?

She had explained that she was divorced, but did her ex-husband still figure in her life? Or was there perhaps someone else? Someone who might whisk her away—marry her, perhaps? He felt the stirrings of resentment against the man. Pity if that should happen—they needed a nurse of her calibre in the practice.

Who are you kidding? That's not only why you want her to stay. The thought manifested itself from somewhere so deep within him that it scarcely registered. He swore softly under his breath. She was an attractive woman, but surely he couldn't be—

Impatiently he smothered the thought, put the guard in front of the flickering remains of the log fire and took himself off to bed.

CHAPTER TWO

IT FELT good to be in uniform again. Gemma slipped the navy blue belt round her waist and fastened the elaborate silver buckle. She was reminded as she fastened it that it was the last present her parents had combined to give her when she had qualified ten years ago. They had parted soon after.

Theirs had been an unhappy marriage, only held together for her sake until she had been safely embarked on her career. But as a small child she had been aware of the cracks. Their parting had been full of recriminations and bitterness. Even their love for Gemma had been tainted towards the end because she had tried to act as a go-between and had only succeeded in upsetting them both.

They had both moved overseas—her mother to New Zealand to marry a sheep farmer, her engineer father to South America with his new partner. They kept in touch, exchanged letters, rare phone calls, Christmas and birthday cards, but Gemma no longer felt secure in their love.

It was a tenuous, remote thing. There was no one to give her a hug of reassurance...they had never even clapped eyes on their granddaughter.

My poor baby, she thought, no caring grandparents and an immature father who visits erratically, and is either noisily cheerful or painfully morose. In the latter mood he would make it plain that he was visiting only out of duty. Would he still make the effort to visit now that they were living in Dorset, and would Daisy mind if he didn't?

Probably not. Her reaction, when Gemma had explained that Daisy might not see so much of him, had been astonishingly calm and untroubled. 'P'raps,' she'd said, in her grown-up, thoughtful fashion, 'Daddy won't be so cross when he takes me out if he doesn't see me very much.'

Gemma had felt bound to defend him. 'But Daddy isn't always cross,' she'd said, 'and when he is, I expect it's because he's got a lot on his mind. He's a very busy man.'

Daisy had given her one of her clear, frank looks, with eyes as green as her own, and had said matter-of-factly, 'You're busy, too, but you don't get cross like he does.'

Gemma said, 'Oh, Daisy, I do love you.' And with a hug and a kiss the conversation had ended.

Reliving that conversation, she thought, It's a miracle that Daisy is such a happy and normal child. Her heart swelled with pride in her practical, sensible little daughter.

She snapped out of her reverie. She had heard Daisy go downstairs a while ago, and when she arrived in the kitchen a few moments later she found her concentrating on pouring flakes into a bowl, her small hands precariously juggling with the large packet.

In a rather sketchy fashion she had dressed in the clothes that Gemma had put out the night before.

She greeted her mother with a beaming smile out of a shining, clean face. 'Hurry up, Mummy, I don't want to be late for school and you musn't be late in your new job.'

Gemma dropped a kiss on the top of her head as she mechanically rebuttoned her cardigan in the right order, and then began slicing a banana onto her flakes. 'We won't be late, love. I can't take you to school before half past eight—there won't be anybody there.'

Daisy squinted at the clock and her lips moved, mouthing, 'Big hand, little hand.' She crowed suddenly, triumphantly. 'The small hand's on the eight and the big hand's a little way past the twelve, so it's just past eight o'clock.'

'Well done, love.' Gemma gave her another kiss and a hug. 'We've bags of time to get to school.'

Olivia Mallory was behind the reception desk when Gemma arrived at the surgery at ten to nine. The waiting area was about a quarter full.

'The calm before the storm,' said Mrs Mallory with a smile, waving her hand over the waiting room. 'These are the patients by appointment. The hassle begins at half nine when the emergency non-appointment list starts. Sam's taking that this morning so be prepared for a few extra dressings and blood tests over and above the list I've prepared for you.'

She handed Gemma a sheet of paper with several names on it and a sheaf of forms detailing blood tests required. 'Booked in bloods to do from yesterday, and three cervical smears. Knowing that I would be covering

Reception in Ellie's absence, they were all due to be done by James or Sam, but now thank God, you're here so, bingo, they're all yours.'

Gemma glanced down the list—one of the bloods was booked for nine, another for nine-fifteen.

'Are any of them here yet?'

'Ben Ashley—he's the elderly chap with the red scarf sitting in the front row. He's down for nine-fifteen, but he's always early. Shirley Lowe's your nine o'clock, but by the time she gets her lot off to work and school she's likely to be late. If I were you I'd see Ben first. I'll explain to Shirley if she turns up while he's still with you—she won't mind.'

She gave Gemma a lovely smile, very like her son's, and pushed a stray, greying lock of hair back from her temple. 'It *is* good to have you aboard, Gemma. Do you think you can find your way round the treatment room?'

Gemma nodded. 'Yes, after the comprehensive tour you gave me yesterday I certainly can, and I can't wait to get cracking.'

'Then good luck on your first morning, my dear. Don't hesitate to call if you need me. I can always leave the desk for a few minutes.'

Ben Ashley was chatty and curious about Gemma's reasons for coming to Blaney St Mary, and was intrigued when she explained that she had inherited Cherry Tree Cottage from her great-aunt.

'Nice lady, Miss Rivers,' he said. 'Always ready to pass the time of day when she was here. Can't think why she wanted to go galli-vanting abroad so much.'

Gemma, sidestepping the invitation to gos-sip, slid a needle smoothly into a prominent brachial vein and said, 'You've got wonderful veins, Mr Ashley, like those of a much younger man.'

Ben looked pleased. 'I'm good for another few years, then. That's what I keep telling the doc, but he insists on me having these blood tests every five minutes.'

'That's to keep track of your diabetes,' Gemma explained.

The old man snorted. 'Diabetes! Had it for years. It don't give me any bother so long as I keep taking the tablets.'

Gemma forbore to say that that was because his medication was being kept under close check and the dosage altered if necessary. She withdrew the needle, released the pressure strap and pressed a gauze pad over the small puncture.

'There we are, all done for another four weeks. See you next month, Mr Ashley.'

Gemma followed Mr Ashley out into the waiting room and called for Mrs Lowe.

'She's just arrived,' said Mrs Mallory, 'but she's gone to the loo. I'll send her in directly.'

There was a tap at the treatment room door a few minutes later and a breathless Shirley Lowe entered, apologising profusely. She was a tall, statuesque, handsome woman with a mop of untidy black hair streaked with grey.

'Sorry about that,' she said. 'Have to keep on spending a penny. Dr Sam thinks I may have an infection, though he's tested my urine and found nothing.'

'Sometimes a urine test doesn't reveal an infection, but a blood test does,' explained Gemma. 'And it may point to a specific bug that's causing the problem.'

'And if it doesn't?' asked Mrs Lowe as Gemma inserted the needle and drew up a syringe full of blood.

'Then we have to look for possible mechanical reasons for the frequency.'

'Could a prolapse—you know, of the womb—cause me to want to keep spending a penny? I do sometimes feel as if I'm bearing down.' Her voice trembled, her cheeks reddened.

Surely she couldn't be shy, thought Gemma as she squirted the blood carefully into several glass vials, ready for despatch to the hospital laboratory. She'd had five children, and seemed a sensible, practical person. Obviously she suspected that she might have a prolapse— so why hadn't she mentioned it to Sam when she saw him yesterday? She seemed almost frightened.

Gently she put the question to Shirley. 'If you suspect that you might have a prolapse, Mrs Lowe, why didn't you mention it to Dr Sam? A simple internal examination would have shown whether you have or not.'

Mrs Lowe blew her nose hard and, surprisingly, tears sparkled in her eyes. 'I know it sounds silly,' she said, 'since I've already got five kids, but I'm only in my early forties. Supposing I want more? I don't want to have my womb taken away. I don't want a—what is it, a hysterectomy?' She gave Gemma a watery smile. 'I suppose you think I'm daft, but

I just love having a baby around. The traditional earth mother, my husband calls me.'

So that was what was worrying her. 'But you won't necessarily have to have a hysterectomy,' Gemma explained, 'unless it's a major prolapse, and the fact that you're obviously not in acute pain or discomfort virtually rules that out. A repair to your uterus may be all that is needed.'

Shirley Lowe's face lit up. 'And I could still have another baby?'

'I don't see why not,' said Gemma, but added cautiously, 'Though you would have to be guided by the consultant who did the operation.'

'So what do I do next? How do I go about setting things in motion?'

'Let Dr Sam examine you and confirm that you *have* a prolapse, and he'll make arrangements for you to see a consultant at the hospital. Look, I'll go and have a word with him, see if he can fit you in this morning. I can't promise that he'll be able to see you, but if you don't mind waiting, I'll see what I can do.'

'I don't mind if I have to wait all the morning,' said Shirley joyfully. 'My mum's looking after my youngest, so I've got all the time in the world.'

At the far end of the corridor Sam, his head bent over something he was reading, was coming out of his office as Gemma came out of the treatment room. She hurried toward him.

'Doctor, please, have you got a moment?' she called, her voice sharp.

His head jerked up, his blue eyes blazing brilliantly in the dim corridor lit only by fanlights over the doors. He snapped to attention and gave her a mock salute. 'Yes, ma'am, and good morning to you, too, Nurse.' There was a dry note in his voice, and his lips quirked at the corners in a half smile.

'Sorry,' she apologised as she halted just in front of him, and belatedly wished him a rather breathy, 'Good morning.'

'Not to worry,' he said, and, taking her firmly by the elbow, he steered her in front of him into his office.

'Didn't mean to sound so peremptory,' she said ruefully. 'I just wanted to make sure of getting hold of you before you called in your next patient.'

He was alert immediately. 'Problem?' he asked.

'Rather a request,' said Gemma, and briefly put him in the picture about Shirley Lowe. 'So I wondered,' she added, when she'd finished explaining, 'if it would be possible for you to see her this morning.'

Pushing back the cuff of his shirt, he glanced at his watch. 'Wheel her in,' he said briskly. 'I'll see her before I start emergency surgery.'

'Oh, that's great, she'll be so pleased.'

Sam shrugged. 'Least I can do to set her mind at rest. Besides, if she has got a prolapsed uterus, the sooner I can get her to see someone the better. There's quite a list for gynaecology patients at the General in Shorehampton, and that's where she'll have to go for surgery.'

Gemma pulled a face. 'Tell me about it. It's dreadful in London—every hospital has a list a mile long.' She half turned away. 'Right, I'll fetch her.'

He touched her arm and smiled his stunning smile. 'And by the way, it's Sam—the ''doctor'' bit's only for the patients.'

Gemma dealt with the other booked-in blood, Martin Carter, after she'd sent a grateful Shirley Lowe on her way to see Sam.

Martin was a thin, nervous young man of eighteen who had been seen by Dr Mallory, senior the evening before. Dr Mallory suspected that he might be anaemic and had requested a wide range of tests. Martin's veins, unlike the elderly Mr Ashley's, were flaccid and difficult to find.

'You'll only feel a small prick,' reassured Gemma, when she found a possible vein on the back of his hand and began massaging it to bring the blood to the surface.

'I can't stand needles,' the young man exclaimed, going almost green and looking as if he might faint.

'Would you like a drink of water?' Gemma asked, and fetched a glass from the basin in the corner of the room. Well, at least, she thought, if he's scared of needles, he can't be shooting up hard drugs.

Ten minutes of reassurance and persuasion, and half a glass of water later, Martin allowed Gemma to take the necessary blood. He left a little later, making no secret of the fact that he was greatly relieved that the ordeal was over.

Poor chap, thought Gemma as she disposed of the syringe and gloves. He hasn't got a clue.

If it is anaemia of any sort, he's going to have to go through this on a regular basis.

The rest of the morning fled past. The three booked-in cervical smears were all straightforward, women having regular check-ups. However, midmorning Sam phoned on the internal line to say that he was sending in a patient—twenty-nine-year-old Marian Talbot—whom he had just examined. She was having problems with acute vaginal discharge and dysmenorrhoea.

'These painful periods are rather worrying,' he said. 'I want to eliminate all possible causes. She's nervous and you will need the same tact and understanding that you exercised with Shirley Lowe. I want a vaginal swab and a cervical smear. I've sent her back to the waiting room till you're ready for her. Any problems, get back to me.'

Marian Talbot *did* need a lot of reassurance, but she was sensible and realised that every possible reason for her condition had to be checked out. During the conversation that Gemma had with her, whilst preparing her for her swab and smear, it emerged that she was a single mother, with a three-year-old son, Tim.

Gemma's heart went out to her. This was a situation that she could relate to. 'Where's Tim this morning?' she asked.

'He's with my next-door neighbour, Betty Bond. She's getting on a bit, but she's marvellous with him—she's a retired nurse. She babysits for me sometimes. I'm lucky to have a good neighbour like Betty.'

'You certainly are,' said Gemma with feeling, knowing only too well the problem of finding a reliable babysitter. It flitted through her mind that if Marian was going to need hospitalisation or a long period of treatment for her condition, she was going to need her good neighbour more than ever.

It was late morning before she had time to stop for coffee. With a sigh of relief, she made her way along the corridor to the small but comfortable staffroom. With Olivia Mallory still in Reception she had thought that she would be on her own, and experienced a little flutter of pleased surprise to find Sam there, pouring boiling water into a mug.

He looked up as she entered. 'I bet you're dying for a cuppa,' he said. 'Dad and I have given you a busy morning. What would you like, tea or coffee?'

'Coffee, please, black.'

He poured water into a second mug. 'With sugar?' he asked.

Gemma hesitated.

'Go on,' he said. 'Be a devil. You don't have to worry about putting on an ounce or two. Anyway, you'll soon burn it off. You'll be helping me with the kids' clinic this afternoon. It's like bedlam—you'll soon work off a few pounds.'

Gemma laughed. 'Your mother did warn me, but I'm looking forward to it,' she said, as he handed her a steaming mug. 'I like working with kids. If I'd stayed in hospital, I think I'd have specialised in paediatrics.'

'Thank God for that,' he said fervently. 'Val Prentiss, who'd been our practice nurse for years but upped and married and moved away, loved it, but her successor didn't. I think that's one of the reasons she left after only a few weeks. She just didn't fit in. She was a restless soul—she barely touched down before she was swanning off.'

His mouth curved into a sudden smile, and there was a humorous yet tender expression in his eyes. 'Let us hope,' he said with quiet intensity, 'that *our* encounter is not to be as brief.' He bent toward her and clicked his steaming mug to hers.

Gemma lifted her mug to her lips and took a sip of her coffee. What did he mean by a brief encounter? Was there a *double entendre* there? Was he talking just about work, or implying something more personal? She wouldn't have put him down as a flirt, but... Better put him straight.

Her pulse quickened a little, but she replied coolly, 'There's no chance of that, Doctor. I'm *not* a free agent, I'm not going to go swanning off anywhere. I'm committed *solely* to my daughter's welfare—our home is here now, and as long as she is happy, here we mean to stay.' Had she laid it on too thick?

The teasing expression in his eyes changed—they were suddenly serious. He put down his mug, ran his fingers through his hair and frowned. 'I assumed as much. I'm sorry if I appeared to be a touch over-enthusiastic, but we've been without a nurse for a month and I was, in fact, making a feeble attempt at a joke. I've now seen you in action, and so far I like what I've seen. I—*we*—would hate to lose you.' He produced a faint lopsided smile, and added, 'Am I forgiven?'

They'd been without a nurse for a month— no wonder they were pleased to have her. Gemma found herself staring into his brilliant blue eyes. They met hers steadily. They were neither teasing nor patronising, just honest, innocent like a clear blue sky on a summer's day.

She nodded and gave him a slight smile. 'You're forgiven,' she said.

'Good.' He picked up his mug and and gulped down a mouthful, then looked at his watch. 'Hell, I'd better be off. I'm late starting my rounds.' And with a brisk nod, he turned and left the room.

Gemma stared at his retreating back as he disappeared through the doorway. She didn't quite know what to make of him. Were his words as innocent as he'd suggested, or had he been making a pass at her? He'd tried to make it plain that he wasn't but, then, he would, wouldn't he, seeing her reaction? He was a charmer, that was for sure, and clearly at ease with women, but with two sisters, that wasn't surprising.

A little frisson of regret rippled through her that she had stated her position perhaps rather too strongly. Poor man. For a moment he'd looked poleaxed by her vehemence, the expression in his eyes had changed and there had been a flicker almost of—*hurt*? Or had she imagined that?

Surely a man of his age and experience wouldn't be…hurt, simply because she hadn't pulled any punches. Surely he would appreciate her being straightforward and making it plain that her world circled Daisy's, and that anything outside of that just didn't interest her.

She pulled her thoughts up short. Of course he wasn't hurt. She must have misinterpreted his expression. He might be a country GP, but a man with his looks and from a distinguished local family would have any number of social contacts; he probably had a whole retinue of women whom he could and did date. Why the hell should he be in the least affected by a brush-off from a thirty-plus divorcee with a child?

No reason whatsoever, common sense told her. With a snort of self-derision, she dismissed all thoughts of Sam Mallory from her mind and set about topping up her shelves from the stock cupboards and logging her morning's work.

Sam, too, was deep in thought as he drove away from the surgery. Why had Gemma been so fiercely defensive, almost as if she thought he was going to pounce on her? Surely he hadn't been that threatening. All he'd meant to convey was that by the way she had handled the morning's patients she'd already proved that she was a good nurse, and the practice wouldn't want to lose her.

It was a genuine compliment to her professional ability, an acknowledgement that in a few hours she had succeeded in fitting in. Purely a compliment to her professional ability. *Really?* said the taunting voice of his subconscious. 'Really,' he muttered firmly, under his breath.

Shirley Lowe had been very impressed. 'I like your new nurse,' she'd said. 'She was so kind and reassuring when I was trying to explain about being afraid of not being able to have any more babies. She must have thought me absolutely bonkers, but she seemed to understand. I think you've got a cracker of a nurse there, Dr Sam.'

Silently Sam agreed. The word 'cracker' just about described Gemma, he thought, both as a nurse and a woman. Warm and vibrant with her glowing reddish-brown hair and emerald green eyes—and fiercely independent beneath that calm exterior. He liked that, liked it very much.

Not sure where his thoughts were heading, he reined them in sharply. Hey, steady man, you hardly know the woman. Give yourself— give *her*—a bit of space. You know you're a sucker for a pretty woman, even a pretty woman with a six-year-old daughter. Just don't get carried away—there's no hurry, she'll be around for the foreseeable future.

Take things nice and easy, he warned himself as he drew up in front of a small bungalow where he was due to see his first patient. Picking up his surgical case was a signal to switch into professional mode as he made his way up the short garden path. He was all geared to deal with old Mrs Smith's chronic emphysema.

Gemma was finding the euphemistically named toddlers' clinic, which included crawlers of ten months, just as hectic as she had been warned it would be, but she was loving every minute of it.

She had wondered after the conversation she'd had with Sam whether working together might be a bit awkward—but it wasn't. Even before the session had started, any awkwardness that there might have been had been broken when he'd handed her a pink plastic Teletubby apron and, rolling up his shirt sleeves, donned one himself.

Gemma burst out laughing at the spectacle of his tall, lean figure covered in the colourful pinny that barely reached the top of his thighs.

'Don't mock, Nurse,' he said with pretended severity. 'Out of long experience I've learned only too well the hazards of dealing with our smaller customers. There's always something coming out of one end or the other. And as a by-product, of course, my pinny does help keep them amused and relaxed.

And he was dead right, she thought when towards the end of the session he was examining a tiny infant of eleven months, his narrow, lean hands moving gently over the small body. The baby was fascinated by the shiny plastic, reaching out to touch the garish images as Sam bent over him.

Sam smiled across at the young mother who was looking anxious.

'Barry's doing fine, Jessie,' he said. 'He's very slightly underweight, but that's partly because he's such an active baby. He's not undernourished, there's nothing to worry about, everything's in good working order and ticking over fine.' As if to emphasise the point, Barry jerked and shot out a jet of urine straight at Sam's plastic-covered front.

The baby gurgled, the young mother giggled nervously and apologised. Gemma grinned and handed Sam a tissue.

'There, Jessie,' he said, with a deep throaty chuckle as he mopped himself off. 'As I said, nothing wrong with any of his working parts.' He picked the baby up and handed him to his mother. 'You can get him dressed now, and we'll see him in four weeks' time, unless you're worried about anything before then.'

Sam grinned at Gemma after Jessie and baby Barry had left the cubicle. 'What did I tell you?' he said. 'To be prepared is to be forearmed. Without my precious pinny, I'd be stinking to high heaven before the session finished.'

Gemma inclined her head. 'I bow to your superior wisdom,' she said with a laugh as she left the cubicle and went out to usher in the next and last patient.

This was a pretty little girl of fourteen months, Patsy Jordan, who'd recently had a repair made to a cleft palate. The repair had been successful, but Sam was keeping an eye on her to assess that the slight deafness associated with the damaged palate was not deteriorating. He examined both her ears whilst she sat on her mother's lap, and gave her several simple sound tests. He referred to a note that he'd made on her last visit, then turned to her mother.

'I think, Maeve, we'd better get Patsy seen by the paediatric specialist she was with in Shorehampton General. Nothing dramatic, but I think there's a slight deterioration which could affect her now that she's just started to talk. I'll write and fix something up. You should hear from the hospital quite soon.'

'Will she have to wear a hearing aid?' Mrs Jordan's voice wavered.

Sam said gently, 'That'll be for Dr Rayburn to decide, but better a hearing aid than that Patsy's growing vocabulary should be curtailed because she doesn't hear properly. Makes sense, doesn't it?' He tickled the little girl under her chin and she gurgled happily, then wriggled down off her mother's lap and made a tottering beeline for the gap in the cubicle curtains.

Gemma dived after her and swung her up above her head. Patsy crowed with delight. Gemma planted a noisy kiss on the soft cheek and Patsy bubbled with laughter.

'She's a lovely little girl,' Gemma said as she handed her back to her mother. 'And if she does need to have a deaf aid, as Dr Sam thinks she might, they're very discreet these days, and Patsy's curls will hide it. No one will ever know that she's wearing one.'

'Thanks for the back-up. That was a neat endorsement of what I told her,' Sam said a few minutes later when Patsy and her mother had left. 'You're very good at this reassuring lark.' He smiled and glanced at his watch, nestling against the fine, golden, silky hairs at his wrist. He looked up and his eyes met Gemma's. 'It's nearly three—time you went off to meet Daisy from school.'

Gemma looked startled. 'Oh, no! I hadn't realised.' She waved a hand round the toy-strewn waiting room. 'Look, Sam, would it be all right if I fetch Daisy and come back to tidy up? She won't be a nuisance, I promise. She won't go wandering about anywhere.'

'I'm sure she wouldn't, and you must bring her over some time to meet us and let her see where you work, but not today. You've had a full first day, so scoot. I'll tidy up.'

Gemma pulled off her apron. 'If you're sure. Next week I'll arrange to pick Daisy up a little later—apparently there's always someone there till at least half past three.'

Sam smiled. 'You do that. Meanwhile, go, woman, go.'

'Bless you.' She turned and made for the door.

As she reached it, he called, 'And, Gemma, thanks for your help. We make a good team.'

CHAPTER THREE

THOSE last words that Sam had spoken—'We make a good team'—came into Gemma's mind many times over the next couple of days. They *were* a good team. They had worked together smoothly and efficiently, dovetailing in with each other in the toddlers' clinic. There had been no hitches, the atmosphere had been great and the toddlers and their mothers had responded.

Over those two busy days she also felt that she had become part of the practice team as a whole, working harmoniously with both Dr Mallory senior and his lovely wife. They made her so welcome that she already felt that she belonged.

She just hoped and prayed that Ellie Peterson, the receptionist, who, according to Sam, had been with them for yonks, and who was due to return on Friday, would accept her as readily as the Mallorys had. If she didn't, she thought, butterflies fluttering round in her stomach, the situation could be turned on its head. Both Sam and his parents obviously thought the world of Ellie and would value her opinion as a loyal and trusted employee.

Ellie, a pretty, petite woman with a creamy complexion, huge, spaniel-like brown eyes and shining black hair swept neatly back into a chignon, welcomed her with a rather reserved but genuine smile when she arrived for duty just before nine on Friday morning.

'You're Gemma, of course,' she said, leaning across the reception desk to shake hands. 'I'm Ellie. Mrs M.'s been telling me what a tower of strength you've been over the last few days whilst I've been laid low. I'm so glad. The Mallorys are such a lovely family and work like Trojans to keep the practice functioning to their high standards.'

'Yes, I can see that,' said Gemma as she shook Ellie's hand. 'They've been so kind to me, made me feel very welcome.'

Ellie nodded. 'We're one small happy family here, and you'll be one of the family in no time. If Mrs M. approves of you, you're in.'

Gemma laughed. 'Don't the two doctors have any say in the matter? Suppose they disagree?' She still found the thought of the two tall, lean, clever men being bossed by the cuddly Mrs Mallory laughable, though she had seen it happen on her first day.

Ellie chuckled. 'They wouldn't dare,' she said. 'They trust her instinct, and so do I. I've never known it to be wrong, and she's given you the OK, so welcome to Blaney St Mary, Gemma.'

'Thanks. Now I'd better get stuck in—what have you got for me?'

'Quite a list—it's weight-watchers, or general fitness and exercise day, as Sam prefers to call it. He's always at pains to explain that having too much cholesterol and being over-weight are not the same thing—you can be fat outside and thin on the inside. It's being generally fit that matters, and that applies to both the over- and the underweights. Here are their record cards and diet sheets.'

Ellie handed Gemma a pile of cards. 'With a few exceptions, most of the people you will see this morning are the oldies, or mums at home with young children. There's an evening session for people who are at work, but Mrs M. or one of the doctors will deal with them.'

Gemma raised her eyebrows. 'Wow, there are quite a few. Surely there can't be that many people in the village with weight problems?'

'It's bus day. They come in from the sur-rounding hamlets and smaller villages,' Ellie explained, and added, her eyes twinkling, 'and even here in the wilds of Dorset, we're familiar with the current thinking on health and diet—preventing heart disease and so on. Blame it on television. Now, if...'

Her voice trailed off as the door flew open and a man staggered in, carrying a boy who looked to be about six. Blood was pouring down the boy's face from a gash on his fore-head. 'Quick, help me,' the man gasped. 'It's my boy, Brian, he's been cut, he ran into the greenhouse door.'

The boy lay in his arms, limp and apparently unconscious.

'Bring him through here,' said Gemma briskly, leading the way to the treatment room. She called over her shoulder, 'Ellie, get one of the doctors.' Ellie was picking up the phone even as she spoke.

'Put Brian on the couch,' Gemma directed the distraught man.

She grabbed a handful of tissues from the dressings trolley and mopped up some of the blood, which was obliterating one side of the child's face, praying that his eye had not been injured. With glass you never knew. It appeared undamaged. She heaved a silent sigh of relief and with a fresh handful of tissues continued to wipe away more of the blood.

Sam arrived as the boy moaned and began to come to. The bleeding was easing off, no longer pouring, though still oozing freely.

Brian suddenly opened his eyes wide and stared at Sam. He looked puzzled, but both his pupils were normal and equal, Gemma and Sam noted with relief. They were both aware that a skull fracture was always a possibility with a head wound, especially if a patient was unconscious.

'Looks like he fainted with shock,' Sam murmured, as he pulled on plastic gloves. He bent over the boy. 'Brian, it's Dr Sam—can you hear me?'

They heard a whispery, 'Yes.'

'You've hurt yourself,' Sam said gently. 'Daddy's brought you to the surgery. I'm just going to look at this cut you've got on your head.'

Brian whimpered. 'Daddy.'

His father took his hand. 'It's all right, son, I'm here.' He looked at Sam and pleaded in a low, shaky voice, 'He's going to be all right, isn't he? He's bleeding so badly.'

Sam gave him a quick glancing smile. 'Head wounds do bleed profusely, Hugh, even quite small ones. I'll be able to tell you more when I've cleaned him up.' He turned to Gemma. 'Let's have some gauze swabs and forceps, please, Nurse.'

Gemma, anticipating his request, had a receiver, several forceps and a bowl full of swabs and antiseptic at the ready.

With infinite care, in case there were slivers of glass embedded in the damaged tissue, Sam swabbed the wound. Brian whimpered occasionally as he worked, but for the most part seemed reassured by Sam's soft voice and gentle fingers.

'Looks clean,' he muttered after a few moments, dropping the blood-soaked swabs into a receiver that Gemma placed beside him. She handed him another pair of forceps loaded with a dry swab, and he applied a little pressure to the open wound to stem the bleeding. With his other thumb and forefinger, he experimentally eased the two edges of the cut together.

'I think we can get away without stitching this,' he said with a grunt of satisfaction. 'It isn't as deep as we thought at first. So what I'm going to do, Hugh,' he explained to the anxiously hovering father, 'is hold the wound together with fine strips of special adhesive tape.'

He smiled down at Brian, squeezed his small shoulder and said softly, 'Brian, you heard what I was telling Daddy. We're going to mend this cut by pulling the edges of it together. Before I do that I'll put something on your head to make it numb and cold so you won't feel anything very much. Do you understand old chap?'

'Yes.' Then, predictably, he went on in a quavery voice, 'But it won't hurt, will it?'

Sam said evenly, 'It shouldn't do, but it might feel a bit sore so we'll give you a tablet to swallow to help that. But it won't take too long to do—it'll soon be over. Now, are you ready, Brian? Shall we make a start?'

Brian whispered, 'Yes.' He closed his eyes.

While Sam had been talking, Gemma had laid up the dressings trolley with antiseptic and an anaesthetising agent, scissors, gauze swabs, forceps and narrow-strip adhesive dressing tape and a medicine measure containing a junior aspirin.

Brian was given the aspirin, and the local anaesthetic was applied to his forehead and given a few minutes to take effect. Then Sam got to work. Quickly and evenly, keeping the two edges of the wound in alignment, he applied, in criss-cross fashion, the narrow strips of tape that Gemma handed to him.

It was as neat a bit of 'stitching' as she had seen, she thought. 'Nice work,' she murmured, as she covered the injured area with a window dressing so that they could keep an eye on the wound whilst it was healing.

'Thanks.' Sam smiled down at Brian. 'All done, old chap, you were very brave.' He gave the boy a conspiratorial wink. 'I think you deserve something from the sweetie jar—let's see what Nurse can conjure up for you.'

For an instant, his blue eyes, full of warmth and humour, caught Gemma's in a twinkling sideways glance, and she was acutely aware of the sheer masculine charm of the man behind the caring doctor. The glance caught and held briefly and she felt a little dart of pleasure shafting through her and momentarily found herself smiling into his laughing eyes.

The moment passed—it might never have happened. Smoothly transferring her smile to Brian, Gemma reached for the sweetie jar.

While Brian was choosing a brightly coloured lolly, Sam gave Hugh instructions about keeping the boy quiet and warm for the rest of the day. 'And call me at once,' he added, 'if he is sick or there is any change in him that worries you. And give him plenty of fruit juice to drink. Bring him back the day after tomorrow so that I can see how his wound's progressing.'

The rest of the morning flew past, as Gemma weighed and in some cases measured height, advised and reassured. Most of the patients were fighting to lose a few—or many— pounds, but one or two were underweight. Ralph Wyman, forty-eight, was one such patient.

Gemma checked his notes, before calling him in to the treatment room. He was making a long, slow recovery from stomach cancer. The affected part of his stomach had been successfully surgically removed, and he had just completed a course of chemotherapy. He was a writer, a widower and lived alone in an isolated cottage a couple of miles outside the village. Recently he had suffered several small fits, had been diagnosed as mildly epileptic and had had his driving licence withdrawn, hopefully only temporarily till his epilepsy was under control.

'This patient is *seriously* underweight,' Sam had written rather despairingly. 'Please encourage him to eat *anything* that he fancies, particularly food high in carbohydrates and proteins. And advise to eat little and often...this is one patient who can afford to snack between meals. I can't seem to get through to him.'

That, thought Gemma, was surprising. It was difficult to imagine Sam at a loss with a patient, but for some reason he apparently didn't gel with Ralph Wyman. Well, even a doctor as good as Sam Mallory can't win them all, she thought.

She went to the door of the waiting room and called for Mr Wyman, and watched as a tall, thin beanstalk of a man uncoiled himself from his chair and loped tiredly across the room.

He was thin to the point of gauntness, his cheeks sunken, his skin unhealthily pale and dry, his grey hair thinning at the temples. He walked with a stoop, but he produced a rather sweet, weary smile when Gemma invited him to sit down. 'I suppose,' he said wryly, 'that you're going to add your voice to the others and lecture me about eating.'

Gemma grinned. 'That comes within my remit,' she acknowledged gently, 'but I don't think I really need to, do I? *You* know that you're bordering on the edge of malnutrition and making a mockery of the successful operation to remove the growth. You're not apparently suffering from nausea, or having pain when eating—so why don't you eat, Mr Wyman?'

'Never been much interested in food and I forget when I'm writing.'

'And by the time you remember, you're past it—right?'

'Spot on, Nurse. My wife used to keep me tanked up, but...' A shadow passed over his face, and it looked suddenly very bleak.

Gemma's heart gave a jerk of sympathy but, keeping her voice even, she asked, 'How long since your wife died?'

'Three years—seems like yesterday. Thought by moving here away from our circle of well-meaning friends I'd somehow come to terms with it, but I haven't so far.'

'But you didn't bargain on getting ill yourself, did you?'

He pulled a face. 'No, that's for sure.'

'Do you manage for yourself, or have somebody in to clean for you?'

'A Mrs Fairbody descends on me three times a week.' One side of his mouth quirked into a lopsided grin. 'And she is,' he said.

'Is what?' frowned Gemma. 'You've lost me.'

'A fair body…what my mother used to call, a fine figure of a woman.' His weary grey eyes brightened for a moment.

Gemma smiled her appreciation. Thank God he'd managed to hang onto a sense of humour. 'Nice one,' she said. 'Now does she do, or would she do any cooking for you?'

'Been desperate to get her hands on my pots and pans since day one.'

'Then let her loose in your kitchen. Let her spoil you. Tell her you're to have *small*, nourishing dishes at frequent intervals to build you up. Cauliflower cheese, egg custard, stewed fruit, chicken soup, pasta dishes—she'll know what to do, she'll fill up your freezer in no time. You're much more likely to eat if there's something ready to hand.'

Ralph Wyman stared at her in silence for a moment, then drew in a deep breath. 'Is that it?' he said. 'Aren't you going to read me the riot act about making myself eat, and so on?'

She shook her head. Some instinct told her that the time for pussyfooting around with this sad, intelligent man was past. Somehow she had to get through to his self-respect, his sense of self-worth. He may not care if he lived or died—but she did. The time for begging for his co-operation was over.

'What's the point, Mr Wyman? You don't need me to tell you what you should do. If you want to survive, you've got to make yourself eat, or you'll be back in hospital on drip feeds, and that would be a waste of everyone's time and money and set you back months. There isn't any other answer—your cure lies in your own hands.'

His exhausted grey eyes searched her face. 'You pretend to be hard, Nurse, but you really care, don't you?' He stood up, wafer-thin, and leaned across the narrow desk where Gemma did her paperwork. 'At a guess,' he said softly, 'I'd say you weren't a stranger to a share of life's traumas.' He straightened up, squaring his shoulders. 'Right. I take note of what you've said. Thanks for being honest with me.'

He went quietly out of the door, closing it softly behind him.

Gemma gazed at it, deep in thought. Had she been right to take a tough line with the frail, unhappy man who had just passed through it? Should she have tried to coax him a little more, rather than pass the buck to him? Had she stepped out of line, exceeded her brief? Would Sam approve of what she had done?

The door opened slowly and Sam's handsome, corn-bright head appeared round it. 'I did knock,' he said apologetically, his eyes twinkling.

Gemma felt a little ripple of pleasure trickle through her. It *was* good to see him after the grey, sick, sad Ralph Wyman. He glowed with health and positively lit up the room. 'Sorry, didn't hear you. Please, come in. I was thinking about poor Mr Wyman.'

'Poor Mr Wyman is why I'm here,' said Sam. 'I saw him leave, wondered what you made of him. He's on my conscience. I feel that we should be doing more for him. What do you think, Gemma?' He perched himself on a corner of the desk and his eyes, grave now, searched her face intently, trying to read what was there.

She met his gaze frankly. 'I think that he hasn't made up his mind whether he wants to live or die, and until he does there's precious little you or anyone can do for him.'

'You mean, he doesn't care because he is still grieving for his late wife?'

'Yes.'

'Early on I tried to get him to talk about it, but he's an intensely private person. Did you manage to get anything out of him?'

'Just the fact that he misses her dreadfully.'

'Did he actually admit to that?'

'Yes.'

'Well, that's something. He just clammed up on me, virtually told me to mind my own business. Any luck on the eating front?'

'I'm afraid I got rather tough with him—told him it was up to him to play ball with us, otherwise his op and subsequent treatment had been a waste of time. Whether he will or not, remains to be seen. He seemed to be grateful, for what he called, my honesty, but whether it'll have the desired effect I don't know.' She felt her cheeks colour faintly. 'I'm so sorry if I've pushed him too far. I should have consulted with you first—I may have done him more harm than good.'

Sam shook his head. 'No,' he said decisively. 'You looked at him with new eyes and made a clinical judgement. It may have been just what he needed, to be forced to look at himself. Nothing else was working, there is nothing to lose.' He slid off the desk and smiled down at her. 'I trust your judgement implicitly. I place great store by professional instinct backed up by sound knowledge and, quite properly, you acted on yours.'

He crossed the room, but paused at the door. He dropped his voice a notch, and asked rather throatily, 'So, how do you feel at the end of your first week, Gemma—any regrets about joining us?' He raised one eyebrow in a humorous question. A faint smile hovered round his wide, generous mouth.

'None whatsoever,' she replied without hesitation. 'I feel as if I've worked here for years, not barely a week. I feel that I...'

'Belong?' he suggested softly, his eyes holding hers across the width of the room.

She stared into their brilliant blue depths. 'Yes,' she breathed.

Sam gave her a dazzling smile. 'God bless your great aunt Marjorie for bringing you to Blaney St Mary,' he said.

Some timbre in his voice sent a pulse beating madly in her throat. She fought to ignore it, got her breathing under control and smiled back. 'Amen to that,' she said firmly. 'It's the best thing that ever happened to Daisy and me.' Daisy! The beating pulse in her throat, slowed, returned to normal. 'We *both*,' she added, with emphasis, 'feel as if we belong.'

Amusement flared in his eyes—the emphasis on both, hadn't been lost on him. 'Ah, yes,' he murmured, 'Daisy! We've yet to meet Daisy. Why don't you bring her over to say hello after school—I've a gap between surgeries this afternoon. And Mum comes over on a Friday to help Ellie with the week's paperwork, and even Dad may be back from his house calls so she can give us all the once-over.'

'Thank you, she'd like that very much. She's an awfully curious child and full of questions about everything and everyone. I have to give her a blow-by-blow account of all that's happened every day.' She frowned. 'Oh, Lord, does that make her sound as if she's a precocious little monster?'

He laughed. 'Not at all. It sounds as if she's an intelligent, loving little girl who likes to keep tabs on her mum.' He looked at his watch. 'Time I was off—see you later.'

With a half salute, half wave, he whisked himself out of the door and she listened as his long, loping footsteps receded down the corridor.

The rest of the morning passed without incident. Two of her overweight ladies were jubilant at having lost a few pounds, and a bluff, middle-aged gentleman waiting for a hip replacement reached his goal weight and was over the moon.

'At last, to be free of this pain will be a miracle,' he said.

At lunchtime, when the surgery closed for forty-five minutes, Gemma dashed over to the cottage for a snack and to do a bit of tidying up, but returned in time to have a coffee with Ellie before they opened up again. Ellie lived in a small village some miles away and didn't go home to lunch but had a sandwich in the staffroom.

'I have a standing invitation to the Mallorys for lunch but I only occasionally take advantage of it,' she explained with a diffident smile. 'Feel they don't always want me hanging around.'

'Very sensible of you,' agreed Gemma. She took a sip of coffee. 'I suppose your husband doesn't get home for lunch very often—he's something to do with farming, isn't he?'

To Gemma's surprise, the expression on Ellie's gentle face hardened. 'He's out all hours. He deals with farm machinery selling and repairing.' She sounded bitter and resentful and a faint wash of colour stained her pale cheeks. 'I think he thinks more about his beastly tractors than he does about me,' she added with a bleak little laugh.

Not knowing what to say, Gemma remained silent and stared down into her mug. She was totally unprepared for this outburst.

Ellie took a slurp of coffee. 'Sorry, not fair to you, shooting off like that,' she said. 'Didn't mean to embarrass you...unforgivable of me. It's just that sometimes it gets on top of me. He seems so wrapped up in his bloody machinery we just never seem to have time to talk any more. I have the feeling that he's avoiding me.'

Tell me about it, Gemma felt like saying, remembering the last year or so of her marriage to Neil and the fabrications he had made for getting home late.

Instead, she said gently, 'Men and their machines, they're like little boys, aren't they? And most of them are not good at talking, discussing their emotions. Perhaps he would like to talk but doesn't know how to begin.'

'Perhaps.' Ellie clearly didn't believe it for one minute. She pinned a smile on her face and made an obvious effort to pull herself together. 'Now, spill the beans about yourself,' she said. 'Mrs M. tells me that you have a little girl—lucky you.'

'Yes, Daisy, she's six, and I think she's God's gift to the world, but, then, I'm prejudiced. You'll meet her this afternoon. Sam kindly suggested that I bring her in and give her a guided tour so that she's familiar with where I work. He thinks it will be reassuring for her.'

To Gemma's surprise, Ellie blushed furiously and her eyes brightened. 'How like Sam to think of something like that,' she said. 'He's marvellous with children, he's got a way with them.'

'Yes, he certainly has. It was obvious when we did the toddlers' clinic that he has an affinity with children.'

'I think perhaps it's because he is the oldest in the family. According to Mrs M., he was always good with his younger brother and sisters but, then, he's a rather special sort of man, don't you think?' Ellie's voice was full of admiration—and something more besides?

Good Lord, I believe she fancies him, Gemma thought. I wonder if he realises it? I wonder if that's why she and her husband...

Ellie repeated, 'Well, don't you think he's rather special? All women do.' She sounded slightly aggressive.

Tread warily, thought Gemma, and said carefully. 'I don't really know him well enough to comment—after all, I've been here barely a week—but from what I've seen, I think all three Mallorys are rather special.'

Ellie said brightly. 'Yes of course, they are.' But Gemma felt that she had expected a more fulsome answer in praise of Sam, or was the mild-mannered receptionist suspicious of her?

She looked at her watch and with an inward sigh of relief realised that there was no further chance to pursue the subject as it was a quarter to two and time to open for afternoon surgery.

The Friday afternoon surgery was mainly taken up with the small diabetic clinic. During the course of the afternoon Sam sent several patients through to Gemma in the treatment room to be weighed and have urine tests, and in two cases to have dressings renewed to typical slow-healing ulcers—in one case on the toes, in the other on the shin.

She also had to book in some patients to come back on Monday for blood tests. These couldn't be done in the afternoon because they had to be despatched to Shillingbury Cottage Hospital, ten miles away, for laboratory examination before twelve each day.

Sam rang through just after half past two to say that he was sending in the last patient. She was a newly married, newly diagnosed, young diabetic who had recently moved into the area. He wanted her weighed and measured and booked in for a blood test on Monday.

'Here's another chance for you to do your Florence Nightingale bit, Gemma,' he said. 'The poor girl needs bags of reassurance and

TLC. Her name's Cathy Burns, and she's worried that having diabetes will stop her having a baby. Do confirm what what I've told her, that there's no reason why she shouldn't have a healthy baby as long as she sticks to her diet and medication and has regular check-ups.'

'Will do,' said Gemma, impressed yet again by the deeply personal interest he took in his patients.

But when Cathy left twenty minutes later, she was still only partially convinced. Gemma had given her some leaflets about diabetes in pregnancy for her and her husband to read, and had promised that when Cathy came back on Monday for her blood test they would go into the subject in greater depth.

Somehow she must convince Cathy that generally it was safe for a diabetic to have a baby, provided she obeyed all the rules, but quite how she was going to do this she wasn't yet sure. Perhaps there was another young diabetic mother in the practice catchment area with whom she could put Cathy in touch. She would ask Sam and Dr Mallory senior if either of them had a patient who fitted that category.

A few minutes later, pondering on this possibility, she sped up the green to collect Daisy from school and put her in the picture about visiting the surgery.

The visit, though short, had been a great success, Gemma reflected, lying in bed that night waiting for sleep to come. Daisy had been her usual happy, outgoing self, neither pushy nor shy, shaking hands composedly with Mrs M. and Ellie in Reception and later with both the doctors. All of them, experienced professionals that they were, had welcomed her without talking down to her.

Except for the children's corner in the waiting area with its brightly coloured toys and books, there wasn't much to interest a six-year-old girl. But Daisy had jumped at Sam's suggestion that she might like to see the treatment room where her mother worked most of the time. She had been impressed by the gleaming glass and chrome cupboards and dressings trolley, and, curious as ever, had wanted to know what various receptacles and instruments were called, repeating the names after Gemma.

The highlight of the afternoon, however, was when Sam offered her the sweetie jar. He explained that the sweets were kept to offer children who had been brave when they'd had to have something not very pleasant done to them to make them better.

About to dip her chubby hand into the jar, she hesitated and, ever practical, said slowly, 'But I haven't been brave, so is it all right for me to have one?'

Smiling, Sam said, 'It certainly is, Daisy. Let us say that it is because it is the first time you have come to visit—it's a welcome to Blaney St Mary.'

Daisy beamed. 'OK,' she said, and, her green eyes sparkling, pulled out a bright red lolly.

All in all, thought Gemma drowsily, it had been an interesting day to end her first week—meeting Ellie, little Brian with the cut on his forehead, sad, thin Ralph Wyman, Cathy Burns, diabetic, afraid to have a baby...must try and help her...

CHAPTER FOUR

GEMMA surfaced on Saturday morning when Daisy bounced into bed beside her. She opened sleep-bleared eyes and groaned as her daughter burrowed into her and gave her a smacking kiss on the cheek. She gave her a fumbling kiss in return and stroked back the tangle of curls from round the happy little face.

'Hello, darling,' she mumbled, squinting over Daisy's head at the clock—nearly eight. She'd had a wonderful night.

'Hello, Mummy. My room's full of sunshine—why isn't yours?'

First question of the day, thought Gemma. 'Because your room faces east and the sun rises in the east and the earth turns to meet it, and mine faces the opposite direction, west, so I get the evening sunshine,' she explained. 'But if you pull back the curtains, love, we can look at the blue sky, watch the clouds sail by and have a cuddle while we plan what we're going to do for the day.'

'Scrumptious,' crowed Daisy, hopping off the bed and over to the window which overlooked the green. She pulled back the chintzy curtains and bright daylight filled the room. Birdsong filtered up from the front garden through the open casement.

Daisy bounded back onto the bed and curved herself against Gemma. She exhaled a huge sigh of contentment. 'Isn't it funny, Mummy?' she said. 'I like school very much, but I like it when I'm home with you, too, just you and me.'

Gemma felt a warm glow in the pit of her stomach, not just caused by her daughter's neat round bottom which was pushed into it. 'Poppet,' she said, kissing the top of Daisy's head, 'you have the knack of saying the right thing at the right time.'

'What's a knack?' asked Daisy.

To the best of her ability, Gemma explained what a knack was.

Daisy pondered this a moment. 'So it's a nice thing,' she said at last dismissively. She gave a wriggle of excitement. 'So what are we going to do today, Mummy?'

'I thought we'd go into Shillingbourne and explore and do some shopping. With summer on the way, you can do with some new shorts and sandals—you've outgrown last year's.'

Daisy shot up in bed and turned round to look down on Gemma, her face shining. 'Can I choose, Mummy, please, please? I know exactly what sandals I want—they must be red.'

'We'll have to see what we can get, love. There aren't as many shops as there are in London. Shillingbourne's a country market town.'

They had a wonderful day in Shillingbourne, which turned out to be much larger than Gemma had expected and full of graceful old Regency buildings. There were loads of shops, ranging from the high class and elegant to the cheap and cheerful. They found Daisy's red, fashionably chunky sandals in the children's department of Browns, a sort of local equivalent of Harrods. The sandals were pricey, but Gemma didn't mind. They were beautifully made and fitted well, with sensible room for growth.

The shorts, together with a couple of jazzy T-shirts, were purchased from a stall in the market. They were so cheap that Gemma, egged on by Daisy who thought they were 'scrumptious'—apparently the present *in* word in the village school—went wild and bought herself amber drop earrings from the next-door stall. She felt terribly extravagant, but comforted herself with the thought that it was in celebration of their first week in Blaney St Mary.

Just like Daisy's lollipop, she thought, recalling Sam smilingly offering Daisy the sweetie jar in the surgery and explaining that it was by way of being a welcome-to-the-village present. It was a nonsensical, silly thought, and gone in a flash.

They lunched in the sunny garden of an ancient pub tucked away off the high street. After lunch they located the library, joined immediately and chose several books each from the packed shelves. Then they went in search of the leisure centre and registered as members of the adults' and children's swimming clubs.

The leisure centre was surprisingly well equipped. Daisy, who had been swimming since she was three, was to be allowed access to the junior pool.

Their last port of call, before leaving Shillingbourne, was to the superstore on the outskirts of the town. Gemma, who had so far only shopped at the village post office stores, stocked up on the basics to fill her larder and fridge-freezer.

In the magazine section they found a Walt Disney video on special offer which Daisy had been coveting for weeks. Still feeling in a celebratory mood, Gemma agreed to buy the cartoon on condition that Daisy contributed a minuscule amount of her pocket money toward the purchase.

Knowing that it was one of her mother's few house rules that she use her pocket money for just such luxuries, Daisy joyfully consented.

Both happy and content, they drove home through the winding lanes and steep hills of Dorset in high good humour. They sang enthusiastically—'Twinkle, twinkle little star' and a whole host of nursery rhymes and children's hymns, which were great favourites and still apparently being sung in the village school.

They had just finished singing 'All things bright and beautiful' when they drew up outside Cherry Tree Cottage. To their surprise, Miss Heinman, their next-door neighbour, was limping—badly limping—down the garden path, stick in one hand and clinging onto the cobbled wall between the cottages with the other. She had obviously come from their front door.

She was as white as a sheet and her face was contorted with pain. She looked as if she was about to collapse at any moment.

Gemma was out of the car in a flash and racing over the narrow strip of pavement and up the garden path, reaching the elderly woman just as she began slipping to the ground. She lowered her gently the last few inches and propped her against the wall.

Miss Heinman fluttered open her eyes. 'Thank goodness you've come,' she murmured. 'I've hurt my leg…knee…ankle…I thought…you being a nurse, but I don't want to be a nuisance.'

'You're not a nuisance. I'm sorry I wasn't in. Don't worry, we'll soon get you sorted out.' Gemma turned to Daisy, who had followed her out of the car, and handed her the the bunch of keys that she'd snatched from the ignition. 'Open the front door, love, and then go next door and ask Mr Roberts if he'll bring round Mrs Roberts's wheelchair and help me get Miss Heinman into the house.'

Round-eyed but composed, Daisy took the keys and did as she had been bade. Mr Roberts arrived quickly with the wheelchair, but it took some time for them to get Miss Heinman into the cottage, with Mr Roberts pushing the chair and Gemma supporting the injured leg to ensure that it didn't suffer further damage.

Once inside the sitting room they transferred Rose—as Mr Roberts addressed Miss Heinman—to Gemma's sofa, with her swollen, twisted leg, on cushions. Seeing that she was reasonably comfortable, Mr Roberts left to attend to his invalid wife, who, he explained, got agitated if left on her own. He took the chair with him but promised to bring it back again if it was needed.

'That Dorothy Roberts makes a fool out of Jim,' said Miss Heinman in a quivery but disgusted voice when he had gone. 'She's a whiner—he waits on her hand and foot.' She winced as Gemma carefully removed the elderly lady's torn stocking and gently examined her leg. 'Not that I can talk, putting you to all this trouble. So what's the damage, Nurse? Will I be able to walk on it soon?'

'Not for a day or so at least, and that's if it turns out to be simply a twisted knee and a sprained ankle. If it's anything worse—'

Miss Heinman interrupted, 'Oh, my dear, do you think it might be worse? How infuriating.' Her colour was improving now that she was off her leg, and she seemed more annoyed than frightened at the prospect of more serious injury.

Gemma said gently, 'I honestly don't know. You may need to have an X-ray to establish the extent of the damage. I'm going to phone the surgery and ask one of the doctors to come and have a look at it. Meanwhile...' She turned to Daisy who was standing quietly by, watching what was going on with keen interest. 'If you would fetch some towels from the linen cupboard, love, and then fetch the freezer bag from the car, we'll give Miss Heinman the ice treatment.'

'What's that when it's at home?' asked Miss Heinman as Daisy went bustling importantly off on her errand, clearly thrilled to be helping.

Gemma explained that it meant packing bags of frozen vegetables or ice cubes round the knee and ankle joints to reduce the swelling.

In no time at all Daisy was back with the towels, and while Gemma spread them on the cushions beneath the injured leg she bustled out to the car and fetched the freezer bag.

The next ten minutes were busy ones. Gemma phoned the surgery and left a message on the answerphone to be switched through to whichever doctor was on duty. She then packed frozen peas and beans round the distorted knee, and ice scrapings from the freezer, collected by Daisy in plastic bags, round the inflamed, swollen ankle.

'I'd like to offer you tea,' she explained to Miss Heinman, 'but it's safer not to, just in case there's something broken and you have to have an anaesthetic. I don't think that's the case, but we'll have to wait for the doctor to give his verdict. But I can give you an ice cube to suck if your mouth is very dry.'

'Thank you, but I'll live,' said Miss Heinman in a rather caustic tone. 'Now, tell me—'

The door bell rang. Gemma said, 'I guess that's the doctor. Daisy, love, you go and let him in.' But before Daisy, who was usually like greased lightning, could move, Sam

Mallory was filling the sitting-room doorway, tall and lean and smiling his wide, warm smile.

'Front door was on the latch,' he said, 'so I let myself in.'

Gemma felt her heart do a curious little flip and found herself returning his smile with a wide one of her own. *Déjà vu*, she thought. It was a repeat of what had happened yesterday when he had come into the treatment room, hard on the heels of poor, sick Ralph Wyman. Now, as then, his thick thatch of corn-coloured hair gleamed and his blue eyes dazzled, and he exuded confidence and reassurance.

'Oh, please, do come right in,' she said. 'It's Miss Heinman you've come to see. She's had a fall and hurt her leg.' She had been kneeling beside the sofa, repositioning the bags of frozen peas and beans, but now stood up.

Sam nodded and crossed the room in a few long strides. 'So you said in your message.' He crouched down beside the sofa and took the elderly woman's hand in his. 'Hello, Miss Heinman. In the wars again? Last time it was a broken arm, and this time your leg. You know, at ninety you lead a very adventurous life. I don't know what my father's going to say about this latest episode.'

The old lady snorted. 'Your father doesn't expect me to keep myself wrapped in cotton wool, any more than he will when he reaches my age. And Mrs Fellows here doesn't think my leg's broken, only sprained or something, and she seems to know what she's about. I hope you appreciate her over in the surgery. As you can see, she and little Daisy have been making me comfortable between them.'

'Indeed they have,' said Sam, flicking a 'well done' smile at Daisy and a slanting, twinkling look up at Gemma. She was flushing slightly. Her elderly neighbour's warm praise surprised her. 'And, yes, I assure you, we do appreciate her in the surgery. Now, tell me how you hurt your leg whilst I have a look at it.'

He bent over the grossly swollen limb and began examining it with firm, experienced fingers, concentrating hard as he exerted a little extra pressure round the swollen knee joint— almost, thought Gemma, as if he could 'see' with his fingers.

While he worked, Miss Heinman explained how she had stumbled at the foot of her garden path, twisted her ankle and banged her knee against the gatepost. 'Which is why,' she said in her rather terse manner, 'I decided to seek Mrs Fellows's help. I didn't think I'd be able to reach up and open my front door, and one garden path is as long as the other. I did not, of course, know that she was out.'

Sam finished his examination and sat back on his heels. 'Well, it's a good job she returned when she did,' he said cheerfully. 'The ice treatment has prevented the swelling getting any worse. As far as I can see, you've sprained your ankle and strained your knee, but there's nothing broken.'

'So no hospital?'

'No hospital, at least at present, but you're either going to have to go to your niece over at Bourne End or have someone in the house with you. I'm going to strap you up with a support bandage from foot to thigh, and I forbid you to put any weight on it for several weeks. You'll have to use two sticks and hop.' He spoke with not altogether pretended sternness. 'Now, what's it going to be—Bourne End or Mrs Carter to live in for a bit?'

Gemma marvelled, as she had several times over the last few days, at the in-depth knowledge that the Mallorys and Ellie had about the patients and their families. There was no such

thing as distancing themselves from their patients in Blaney St Mary. It gave her a definite
glow to think that in time she, too, would be
in that privileged position.

Miss Heinman opted for her niece at Bourne
End because Mrs Carter was going to stay with
her sister for a few days.

'Good,' said Sam, with obvious satisfaction.
'Molly will look after you, and that big, strong
son of hers will make light work of lifting you
when it's necessary.'

It was an hour and a half later before
Gemma and Daisy had the cottage to themselves.

Sam had departed long since to make other
visits, after efficiently strapping up Miss
Heinman's leg, administering a painkiller and
phoning her niece, Molly, to put her in the picture.

'I'll be over to see you at Bourne End on
Monday,' he had promised Miss Heinman, before leaving.

On his way out, without the least facetious-
ness or patronage, he had thanked Daisy for
helping to look after his patient.

Daisy had looked at him with serious emerald green eyes. 'I just did what Mummy told me,' she'd said.

'That's the best sort of help a professional can have,' he'd replied.

Gemma accompanied him to the front door. Dusk was settling over the green. Sam paused on the doorstep. 'Thanks for all you've done for the old lady,' he said. 'Things might have been infinitely worse if you hadn't taken her in hand. I'm sorry you got involved on your day off, but it's the sort of thing that happens in this village.'

'It's one way of getting to know your neighbours,' Gemma replied dryly. 'To date I haven't done more than pass the time of day with Miss Heinman and the Robertses.'

'The villagers, especially the oldies, do tend to keep incomers at a distance till they get to know them. This little episode will build up your Brownie points no end, a sort of baptism of fire. Anyway, thanks for all you've done. Hope you can relax tomorrow and enjoy the rest of the weekend off.'

Sunday started off well. The day was blustery and chilly and punctuated by frequent bursts of heavy rain. But Gemma and Daisy happily dodged the showers to attend the eleven o'clock special children's service, held in the ancient little church tucked away just off the green. They were there at headmistress Joy Scott's instigation.

'Do come,' she'd pleaded when Gemma had dropped Daisy off at school on Friday morning. 'It's only held once a month, and most of the school will be there. It's all very informal, more or less conducted by the children themselves, with a little guidance from the vicar and myself. The children read or recite pieces or poems they have chosen.' Her eyes had twinkled. 'Many with only a fleeting connection with Jesus or the bible story, but what the heck? If anyone can understand, *He* can.' With a laugh, she had pointed upwards.

Gemma had been intrigued. 'We'll be there,' she'd promised.

They thoroughly enjoyed the quirky service, which lasted only forty-five minutes, but by the time they had said their goodbyes to Daisy's school chums and their mums, who were there in force, it was nearly half past twelve when they wended their way homewards across the green.

There was a red, low-slung, lethal-looking sports car with a black hood standing outside the cottage.

Daisy said, 'Wow, what a scrumptious car—red, like my sandals.'

Gemma shrugged. 'I can't think of anyone we know with a car like that. Must be somebody visiting the Robertses.'

But as they crossed the road dividing the green from the terrace, the car door opened and a familiar figure climbed out and leaned on the low roof, watching them approach.

Both Gemma and Daisy came to an abrupt halt. This is where the weekend comes apart, thought Gemma, her heart dropping with a metaphorical thump into her stomach.

Daisy said in a small voice, 'It's Daddy.' She slipped her hand into Gemma's.

Gemma breathed in deeply. 'So it is,' she murmured through tight lips.

Neil was the last person she expected or wanted to see. What was he doing in the wilds of Dorset? When she had told him that they were moving to Dorset, he'd intimated that they wouldn't be seeing much of him when they were 'out in the sticks'. Relief had flooded through her. Alleluia, fewer erratic visits.

It would have been different if Daisy enjoyed her outings with him, but she had recently made it abundantly clear that she didn't. He was too volatile, moody, quickly got 'cross', as she put it.

Gemma squeezed Daisy's hand and, trying to put warmth and reassurance into her voice, said, 'Come on, love, let's go and say hello to Daddy.'

Neil was in one of his expansive, showing-off moods. He swung Daisy up in his arms and kissed her noisily. 'Hello, poppet, what do you think of Daddy's new car? We'll go for a spin in her presently.'

'Not in that lethal object in these narrow lanes you won't, especially the way you drive,' said Gemma firmly. She added, hoping that Daisy wouldn't be seduced by the gleaming red vehicle, 'Besides, we've made plans for the day. It was silly to come all this way without making sure that we would be here.'

Neil lowered Daisy to the ground. She moved a step or two towards Gemma, but for a moment hovered uncertainly between them.

Gemma fished the key out of her bag and beamed Daisy a reassuring smile. 'You go and open the door, love, and we'll show Daddy round.'

'OK.' Daisy almost snatched the key from her and hurried up the garden path.

Neil shrugged and a pleased expression replaced the pout that he'd assumed at Gemma's criticism of his driving. For a fleeting moment she experienced a little spasm of pain—regret—in the region of her heart. He looked, she thought, almost as young and handsome as he had on their wedding day, the eternal Peter Pan. If only...

If only he had learned to grow up, accept the responsibility of a wife and baby, instead of running away. But he just hadn't been able to hack it. If he had, they might have still been together providing Daisy with the ideal two-parent background.

Ideal! That was a hoot. Her parents' marriage hadn't exactly been made in heaven.

Neil was saying in a smug voice, 'Didn't think about you not being in. I'm house-partying with some people in Hampshire—business acquaintances, very dull, but useful. Realised that it was practically next door to you so excused myself to buzz over. Have to get back for drawing-room tea—they're an old-fashioned lot—but I'm all yours till then.'

'Lucky us,' muttered Gemma drily but softly so that Daisy wouldn't hear the irony in her voice. 'You'd better stay for lunch.' She turned and marched up the path, leaving him to follow.

'Happy to accept your gracious offer,' he said, close on her heels.

For Daisy's sake, Gemma worked hard at making Neil's visit a success.

It poured with rain and they were unable to make their planned walk to the top of Round Hill, much, she thought, to Neil's relief. He was a city man, from his sleek designer haircut to the soles of his expensive shoes. As walking was out, they sat round the kitchen table and played board games.

Neil was at his charming best, fulfilling his role of the caring father so successfully that Daisy, who had been rather subdued over lunch, visibly began to relax and enjoy herself. It was lovely to see her giggling and behaving as a six-year-old should, instead of being guarded and watchful as she often was in his presence. If only he was always like this when he visited. If only…

He left just before four, full of promises about visiting again soon. The rain had stopped and a washed-out sun peeped out between a gap in the clouds.

Empty promises? wondered Gemma as she and Daisy accompanied him to the gate. 'Do phone before you decide to come,' she reminded him, and at the risk of spoiling the rapport of the afternoon added, 'and, please, remember what I said about not taking Daisy out in that death trap.' She glanced at the sleek red car standing at the kerb. 'I mean it, Neil.'

He shrugged. 'Don't worry, we'll think of something, won't we, poppet?' As he had when he'd arrived, he swung Daisy up into his arms and gave her a resounding kiss, before setting her down on the ground. Then, to Gemma's utter astonishment, and before she could take evasive action, he put his arms round her, drew her close and aimed a kiss at her mouth, which she averted by turning her head to one side so that it landed just below her ear.

He let her go so suddenly that she rocked on her feet as she staggered back.

Daisy squeaked in a trembly, accusing little voice, 'You *kissed* my mummy. You *never* kiss Mummy.'

'Well, so I did,' he said, sounding pleased with himself, ignoring Daisy's shocked surprise. And with a smirk he turned on his heel, crossed the pavement, lowered himself into the death trap, noisily gunned the engine into life and drove off at a cracking pace.

Gemma seethed but kept a rein on her temper—Daisy was already confused enough. She laid a comforting and protective hand on her small daughter's back and propelled her up the path toward the cottage. There was going to be a hell of a lot of explaining to do. Blast you, Neil, blast and damn you for spoiling things yet again.

Sam, returning from an emergency call-out to a baby with a middle-ear infection and cruising slowly up the other side of the green, witnessed the entire episode.

He tried to interpret what he'd seen. Who was the idiot who'd taken off at nought to sixty in the ten-mile-an-hour restricted zone round the green? The idiot who'd made a fuss of Daisy and had attempted to kiss Gemma?

Even from a distance he could have sworn that she hadn't wanted to be kissed, the way she had staggered back from the man.

What sort of a *friend*, if that's what he was, would try to force a kiss on a woman in broad daylight?

He stopped the car and stared across at Cherry Tree Cottage. Were they all right, Gemma and Daisy? They had somehow looked vulnerable as they had walked up the path. Or had he imagined that? Should he find some excuse to call on them? After all, Gemma worked for the practice. OK, she'd only worked for them for a week, but just the same…

'God help me,' he muttered. 'I'm getting as bad as Dad, doing the paternal caring bit. Keep your distance, Mallory, she wouldn't appreciate you butting in one bit.'

He sighed heavily, and with uncharacteristic clumsiness and a clash of gears cruised back to the surgery.

CHAPTER FIVE

THE week following Neil's disturbing visit had been a busy one for Gemma.

She and Daisy paid a flying visit to Shillingbourne after school on Monday afternoon to buy curtain material, paint and wallpaper to redecorate Daisy's room. It needed doing, but it was more a gesture on Gemma's part to reassure Daisy that all was well. She had been considerably rattled by Neil's silly behaviour on Sunday.

Daisy didn't refer to the kiss, but had been thoughtful and quiet when he'd left and had followed Gemma about like a shadow whilst she was preparing supper, occasionally giving her a hug. Gemma had given her hug for hug, read an extra bedtime story and suggested the trip into Shillingbourne the following day.

The shopping trip worked wonders, and Daisy, who had still been rather subdued when Gemma had left her at school on Monday morning, was by that evening her usual bubbly self.

It had been a busy week at the surgery, too, as they got to grips with a mystery bug which was making the rounds.

Friday was no exception.

Gemma was in the middle of a long list of bloods when Sam appeared in the treatment room between patients. On account of the bug, his house calls had doubled and she had seen little of him over the last few days. The semi-retired Dr Thorn, who lived in a neighbouring village, had been covering much of his surgery work, but wasn't on duty that morning.

Sam greeted her with a tired smile without its usual dazzle, and lines round his mouth were etched deep. Amazingly, though, his blue eyes remained as brilliant as ever.

Her heart went out to him. Astonishingly, a curious desire to hug him, as she hugged Daisy, swept over her. She squashed the outrageous desire and said softly, 'You look exhausted. Can't you get someone else in to help?'

'Bob Carstairs is covering tonight, as well as Saturday and Sunday. He's a locum in a million, and dear old Richard Thorn is covering tomorrow's calls so I'll be off the hook for much of the weekend.'

'Good, you'll be able to go to bed and zonk out.'

'Tempting,' he said, his smile widening, 'but what a waste of time. There are better things to do than sleep.'

Like wining and dining some gorgeous female and dancing the night away, thought Gemma savagely. The savageness of the thought shook her. What the hell was she thinking about? What was it to her whom he wined and dined? She looked pointedly down at her watch.

'Sorry,' Sam said at once. 'Enough chat, you're busy. Can you fit in another blood, please, and a urine test and do a throat swab?'

He handed her some lab forms. 'It's a young woman, Alison Graves. She's new to the area and not very communicative. I haven't got any notes for her. I'll have to ask for them to be faxed through from her last GP. She's presenting with a range of symptoms that could be anything from glandular fever to something more obscure. I want wide-spectrum blood tests, and her urine tested for the obvious—glucose, blood, pus, and so on. I've given her a specimen pot and she should be in the loo, producing a specimen, right now.'

He frowned. 'I rather think we might be looking for one of the autoimmune diseases in its infancy. She complains of feeling the cold, especially in her hands and feet, indicating a circulation problem, Raynaud's probably, which we can do something about. And I thought I could detect a few blemishes across her cheek-bones, which might indicate... But they were very faint. See what you think, Gemma. I'd be grateful for any feedback you can give me. The sooner we can get her sorted, the better.'

'Well, I'll just about manage her before twelve, if...' She raised her eyebrows and inclined her head toward the door.

Sam laughed. 'I'm gone already.' he said.

At the end of her list, Gemma called Mrs Alison Graves in from the waiting room. Alison was tall and skinny, with lank, long, badly tinted fair hair. She was heavily made up.

With ill grace she slouched down in the chair that Gemma offered and handed her the pot containing her urine specimen.

'Dunno why the doctor's going to all this trouble,' she grumbled. 'I thought he'd just give me a tonic or something, so I can get on with my life—if there is any life in this God-awful place. I've just moved, for heaven's sake. That's why I'm so bloody tired.'

'I know exactly how you feel,' Gemma replied with a smile, as she dipped a test strip into the urine. 'I've not long moved myself—it's an exhausting business. But as Dr Sam's seeing you for the first time, he needs to find out if there's any other reason for the symptoms you describe, before prescribing anything. He's a very thorough doctor.'

'Yeah, and cool and dishy with it,' said Alison, with a hint of animation.

Yes, cool, dishy and caring, thought Gemma as she examined the multicoloured testing strip. Everything was negative. 'Well, you'll be glad to know that that's clear. Now, if you'll take off your jacket and pull up your sleeve, I'll take some blood and we'll get it off to the lab for examination. That may give us a clue as to why you're not feeling a hundred per cent.'

She had no problem finding a prominent vein under the bright lights of the treatment room, and was easily able to slide in a needle and take as much blood as she needed to fill the numerous specimen bottles she had lined up.

When she had completed the operation, and whilst Alison, her head slightly bent, was busy rolling down the sleeve of her blouse she took the opportunity to surreptitiously inspect her face. Yes, as Sam had thought, illuminated by the bright lights, though almost concealed beneath the heavy make-up, were the faintest of blemishes across her cheek-bones and the bridge of her nose.

Telangiectasia—sometimes called the butterfly rash—typified certain immune diseases. Sam's hunch had been right. Alison Graves was suffering from more than simple tiredness. With a little flutter of pleasure, she realised what a compliment he had paid her by asking for her opinion, just as he had with Ralph Wyman. It gave her a really warm feeling of being wanted and useful, but, then, that was typical of the whole set-up here at Blaney St Mary.

After seeing Alison out and parcelling up the morning's specimens for collection later, she looked at her watch. It was too late to see Sam now and pass on her findings—he would be out on his rounds. She would have to tell him this afternoon during the toddlers' clinic. The knowledge that they would be working together after nearly a week of seeing so little of him gave her a curious little fizz of pleasure.

Although it was after twelve, she decided that she must have a coffee to sustain her till lunch time. Ellie was in the staffroom, also taking a late break.

'Mrs M.'s holding the fort,' Ellie explained. 'It's been like a madhouse out there this morning, what with the phone going non-stop and people going on holiday wanting to book for various jabs. Not to mention the hay fever sufferers booking in for their anti-allergy jabs. You're going to be busy on those next week.'

'Oh, well, that's par for the course, especially at this time of year,' replied Gemma, spooning coffee into a mug. She poured on boiling water and with a sigh of relief sat down in one of the comfortable old armchairs next to Ellie.

'But I think the bug may be on the wane,' said Ellie. 'Fewer of the calls seem to have been in connection with that this morning, though I haven't done a proper count, so keep your fingers crossed.'

'I certainly will,' promised Gemma, 'Both Dr M. and Sam are looking pretty ragged— they're working flat out.'

Ellie peeped at her over the rim of her mug. 'Yes.' Her cheeks flushed slightly. 'I think Sam in particular looks tired. He's been bearing the brunt of it, he's so protective of his father.'

'Tries to be,' agreed Gemma. She glanced at Ellie's flushed cheeks. Not for the first time she wondered if Ellie had a thing about Sam. A little voice inside her hoped not, but she didn't know why. 'But Dr Mallory's been working his socks off too. The only time I've seen him lose his rag was when Sam offered to do some of his calls as well as his own— the old doctor blew his top.'

'Yes, well, he would, wouldn't he?' said Ellie. 'He's such a dear. Sam's going to be just like him one day, don't you think?' She sounded rather wistful, hopeful that Gemma would agree.

'Well, he could do worse,' said Gemma drily. Then, to change the subject, she asked, 'Doing anything nice over the weekend?'

Ellie pulled a face. 'Visiting my in-laws in Bournemouth. It'll be ghastly. Dave's not looking forward to it either. They never let up, but it's been ages since we visited. If only...'

Wondering if Ellie wanted to talk, yet not wanting to pry, Gemma said cautiously, 'What do you mean, they never let up?'

'About me not producing a baby. As if it's my fault. My God, if only they knew how much I wanted one, only I can't... We can't...' She blinked back tears from her brown eyes and compressed her lips.

Gemma couldn't keep the surprise out of her voice. 'But surely, that's none of their business?' She reached out and touched Ellie's arm. 'I'm so sorry.'

Ellie stood up abruptly and took her mug over to the sink and began washing it. 'I'm sorry, too, coming apart like that, but you're such a good listener and it is nice to have someone near my own age to talk to.' She blew her nose hard and started toward the door. 'Must go now or Mrs M. will be sending out a search party,' adding, as she stood in the doorway, 'you don't know how lucky you are to have Daisy.'

'Oh, but I do,' Gemma said softly, and then went on, 'Ellie, if you think it would help to talk, I'd be only too glad to lend an ear.'

Ellie produced a watery smile. 'Thanks, I'll hold you to that.' Then she whisked herself out of the room.

Gemma made a point of getting back early from lunch to prepare the room for the toddlers' clinic. It took time to distribute the toys, set up the weighing and measuring equipment and lay up a basic trolley in the examination cubicle. It was her second toddlers' clinic. Her spirits, which had been a little low following Ellie's disclosure, soared.

She was on her way back from Reception with a formidable pile of records when Sam caught up with her, taking her by surprise.

She breathed out a startled, 'Oh.' She quickly recovered herself and added, 'You're early.' Then she asked suspiciously, 'Have you had lunch?'

He chuckled. 'You're as bad as Mum, always worrying about the inner man, but, yes, thank you, I have eaten. Finished my visits quicker than I expected.' He glanced sideways at her, his blue eyes twinkling, laughter lines deepening round his half lowered lids.

'We mothers tend to worry about things like that,' she said primly. She had no idea why, but it was suddenly important to remind him that she was a mother.

'Touché!'

They reached the clinic room, and he pushed open one side of the double doors and flattened himself against it. 'After you,' he said, his voice suddenly husky.

'Thanks.' There was a sudden tenseness between them. She found herself trying to make herself as small as possible as she slid past him, but with her arms full she was unable to avoid brushing against his chest. She shrank some more. He breathed in sharply—or had she only imagined it?

'Here, let me.' His voice was gruff, deeper. He took the records from her, his hands touching her bare inner forearms as he scooped them up. The soft flesh tingled. He dumped the files on her desk, then slowly turned to look at her. For a timeless, breathless moment their eyes met and held in a vibrant silence.

There was about a yard separating them. With a step he closed the gap. 'Gemma!' He lifted his hands as though to cup her face. Cup her face... Kiss her... Her eyes still locked with his, she took half a step backwards.

Slowly he let his hands fall to his sides. Then he, too, stepped back a little. The merest shadow of what might have been a smile touched the corners of his mouth. He closed his eyes for a second, cleared his throat and said very softly, 'I can't explain that, Gemma. I just know there's been something...' Palms up, he spread his long, narrow hands eloquently. 'Something since day one, the day we met, when you appeared in the surgery and offered to help. I'm sorry. Have I embarrassed you, scared you?'

His eyes were as brilliant as ever, but no longer dancing. they were thoughtful, serious, as they were when he was dealing with a distressed patient.

Gemma's heart pounded against her ribs, her mouth went dry, her thoughts raced. Should she make a joke of it, laugh it away? It had only been a look after all. *Only*! Her mind was empty of jokes and she could no more laugh than fly.

She stared at him, as if seeing him for the first time—taking in his leanness, his height, the high forehead and the thatch of bright, fair hair springing from his temples, the darker, thick, straight brows, the patrician nose and the firm yet tender mouth.

He was almost too perfect, she told herself. It was difficult to find a flaw in the man, not just physically but in his temperament. But there must be one.

But she didn't want to find a flaw! Perhaps there was the occasional man who wasn't flawed. Something stirred deep within her—a longing, a hope, a joyful awareness, a strange sensation of elation. It had been so long since…

She tried to clear her throat. 'You didn't scare me or embarrass me.' She went on firmly in her normal voice, 'No, not at all, but…'

'But…what do we do about it?'

He didn't need to elaborate further. It couldn't be pushed away, ignored—it was too significant. She kept her voice level. 'What, indeed?'

'Talk?'

'I think we must, but when… There's Daisy…Daisy!' She looked at him, a thousand questions in her eyes.

His voice was gentle. 'I haven't forgotten Daisy—she's the chief reason we must talk,

Gemma. Can I call tonight casually—as a neighbour, a friendly visit?'

There was a hum of voices and the sound of footsteps in the corridor.

There were a dozen reasons why he shouldn't, but many more why he should. It was an unreal situation. Feeling as if she were caught up in some fantasy, Gemma nodded. 'About eight. Daisy stays up till half past on a Friday, but I want her to know that you're there.'

'Not arrive like a thief in the night,' he murmured, as a knock came at the door. 'I'll be there.'

Gemma forced herself to concentrate on her work. She helped mothers undress and dress small bodies; she weighed, measured, reassured and administered injections with her usual calm efficiency. Sometimes she assisted Sam with an examination when a child was being difficult and the mother unable to cope.

They were almost at the end of the clinic, and Sam was examining his last small patient in the cubicle, when a young chap in tattered jeans and a scuffed leather jacket suddenly appeared in the waiting room. He was awkwardly carrying a tiny child who looked to be about a year old. The infant was grizzling, a low, exhausted grizzle that told Gemma it had been going on a long time. Skinny little bare legs were drawn up to its little pot belly, visible between a nappy that stank to high heaven and a too small, grubby jumper.

The young man said, 'They told me out there to bring 'im in 'ere. Can you stop 'im crying? 'E's bin doing it all night.' He thrust the bundle at Gemma. Wordlessly she accepted the pathetic little creature from him and cuddled it to her. 'Oh, an' they said to give you this.' The young man, who looked to be in his teens, handed her a temporary resident's form.

'Name: Gaz Formby', Gemma read. *Gaz?* Date of birth... She stared at it in disbelief. The infant was twenty months old, not twelve as she'd guessed. It was seriously underweight. 'And you are Mr Formby?' She spread a paper sheet on the desk and carefully laid the baby down. In one practised movement she removed the filthy nappy, and with moist wipes began cleaning up the tiny sore bottom.

'Naow, my name's Steve Beck. I'm 'is dad but 'e's got 'is mum's name, only Tracy's not well, like, so she's stayed 'ome.'

'Home being a farm near Bourne End,' said Gemma, glancing at the address on the TPR form. The name rang a bell and she recalled that Bourne End was the village where Miss Heinman had gone to stay with her niece. Gently she wrapped Gaz in a small blanket, then sat down behind the desk and cuddled him on her lap. The grizzle died down to a whimper. 'Is the farm warm and comfortable?' she asked.

'No, it ain't,' said Steve truculently. 'Anyway, we don't live in the farmhouse but in a grotty caravan in the yard. Tracy's uncle owns the farm and caravan, lets us stay in it in return for 'elp about the place. It's a dump, but better than nothing.'

As Steve was talking, Sam was showing the last mother and toddler out of the cubicle.

He crossed over to the desk and looked down at the now almost quiet infant, lying in Gemma's arms. Gently he touched a sallow little cheek, then looked up at Steve. 'Would that be Alf Formby's pig farm?' he asked.

'Yeah,' replied Steve, sounding defensive.

'You're right, that caravan's pretty grotty. It must be difficult to manage, especially with this little chap.' He smiled at Steve and then at Gemma. 'OK, Nurse, let's have…'

'Gaz,' she said, holding back a grin. It was such an odd name for such a tiny scrap of humanity.

Sam clearly agreed with her as his eyes, glinting with humour, met hers. 'Gaz,' he said without a tremor. 'In the cubicle so that I can have a look at him.' He moved across the room and Gemma followed. Steve stayed where he was. Sam paused. 'Aren't you coming, Mr…?'

'Beck, Steve Beck.' Steve shook his head. 'I'll wait 'ere if it's all the same to you—I'm a bit queasy like.'

Sam gave him a reassuring smile. 'Fair enough. I'll give you a run-down when I've finished,' he promised.

Fifteen minutes later he was explaining to Steve that he was going to admit Gaz to the paediatric ward in the cottage hospital at Shillingbourne for assessment and investigation.

'There are several things that could be wrong with your son,' he explained to an obviously bewildered young father. 'It could be simple colic, giving him a pain in his guts, or it could be something more complicated than that. He will have to have scans and tests to determine whether there is anything seriously wrong. He's also very undernourished and needs a special diet to reverse that condition.'

'When will 'e 'ave to go in, then?'

'I want to get him admitted immediately. I'll arrange an ambulance straight away. You can go with him, although you'd have to find your own way back, or follow on in your car— you've got some sort of transport?'

'Van. But what about Trace? She'll be gutted if I don't get back to tell 'er what's 'appened.'

Sam said, 'I'll go over and see her, but it won't be till after my surgery which is due to start shortly—that'll be about six. In the meantime, I'll try to get in touch with Alf Formby and ask him to give her a message.'

Steve said angrily, 'Fat chance. The old bugger don't answer the phone if 'e's out with 'is pigs.'

'There's no need to phone,' interjected Gemma firmly. 'I'll go over to Bourne End and explain the situation to Tracy after I've fetched Daisy from school. Just point me in the right direction.'

'That'd be great. Problem solved.' Sam smiled at her, a wide, special smile that conveyed more than words could possibly have done, and his voice was warm with approval.

A wave of pleasure washed over her at his easy acceptance of her offer. He hadn't sounded surprised or tried to deflect her, but accepted it as he would if his mother had made the offer. She positively glowed, feeling that she was indeed part of the small happy family unit, just as Ellie had predicted.

Half an hour later Gemma and Daisy were on their way to Bourne End. Daisy accepted the change to their usual routine and the reason for it quite happily. In fact, she was thrilled to bits to be visiting a farm, especially a pig farm.

'Will I be able to touch them?' she wanted to know, bouncing up and down with excitement. 'I'd like to, 'specially if there are piglets. I've never seen pigs close up, except on television.'

Bearing in mind Steve's description of the farmer and Sam's rather grim expression when he'd mentioned the name Alf Formby, Gemma tried to cool down Daisy's enthusiasm. He didn't sound the sort of friendly type who would welcome visitors.

'I don't know if the farmer will let us get too close to them,' she cautioned, 'and I don't know how long I'll be with Tracy. I want you to stay in the car while I'm talking to her. We'll see if we can look round afterwards.'

Daisy's pretty little mouth turned down at the corners. 'Oh, Mummy, can't I, *please* just get out of the car. I won't go anywhere, promise.'

Gemma half relented. 'We'll see, love. It might be too muddy.'

Daisy stuck a small red-booted foot in the air and waved it about. 'Oh, Mummy, don't be silly. Don't you remember? I've got my wellies on because it was raining when I went to school this morning.' She was triumphant.

Gemma grinned. 'OK, you win. You can stand outside the car, but you musn't go anywhere until I've finished talking to Tracy.'

They reached the farm at the end of a long rutted lane a few minutes later. It was a low, rambling building which might once have been charming but now looked drab and badly in need of repair. To one side of it across a dirty, untidy yard stood a shabby caravan. It was deep in afternoon shadow and there was something almost sinister about about the whole set-up. There was no sign of life.

No wonder poor little Gaz is so grubby and undernourished, thought Gemma. His parents are little more than children themselves, yet are somehow trying to manage in a place like this.

Daisy was staring, wide-eyed, at the battered caravan. 'Mummy, is *that* where Tracy lives?' she whispered.

'I believe so, love. I'll knock and find out. I'll try not to be too long. You can get out and stretch your legs, but stay near the car.'

'I *think* I'll stay in the car and read my book,' said Daisy with a slight wobble in her voice. 'I can't see any pigs about and I don't think I want to look round *this* farm—it's creepy.'

Gemma gave her a hug. 'I'll be as quick as I can,' she promised.

She got out of the car and crossed the yard to the caravan, wrinkling her nose as she caught a strong whiff of pig.

Fifteen minutes later, she recrossed the yard and let herself back into the car. She smiled at Daisy, though she'd seldom felt less like smiling after her confrontation with Tracy. 'There,

I wasn't long, love, was I?' she said, as she did up her safety belt.

'You were *ages*,' accused Daisy, pouting a little. 'Can we go home now, please? I'm hungry.'

Gemma kissed her quickly on the cheek, before putting the car in gear and starting off down the lane. 'Thanks for being so patient, darling. We'll be home in two shakes of a lamb's tail,' she promised, before it occurred to her that four-legged beasties might not be favourites on the agenda at this moment in time. The Formby farm had definitely been a disappointment. 'And why don't you choose what we'll have for supper tonight as it's Friday?'

Predictably, Daisy, any petulance forgotten, chose baked beans on toast with a sunny-side-up egg on top, her all- time favourite.

Over supper, Gemma struggled to put out of her mind the shocking, unpleasant interview she'd had with Tracy Formby. There was time enough to discuss that with Sam when he called later. Her heart quickened with pleasure at the thought of seeing him, but her stomach churned. Should she tell Daisy that he was coming, or wait for him to arrive? Perhaps the right moment would suddenly materialise when she could mention it casually.

Resolutely, she made herself concentrate on fielding Daisy's questions and asking some of her own. Over pudding, ice cream and mashed banana, another favourite, she asked what homework project Daisy had been given to do over the weekend.

Daisy's chubby little face lit up. 'We've got to draw a coloured picture of the front of our house and count the windows in it and 'scribe it in words,' she said. 'I'm glad. I like drawing and writing.' She half slid off her chair. 'Can I go and count the windows now, please?'

'Finish your pudding first, love, and then we'll both go and count them.'

They stood in the garden a few minutes later, looking up at the front of the house. Daisy counted five windows. One each side of the front door, the sitting room and the dining-room windows, and three above tucked under the gabled roof, the main bedroom, landing and bathroom.

Daisy slipped her hand in Gemma's and sighed contentedly. 'I *do* like living here, it's much nicer than London. My teachers are nice and the people are nice at your surgery, aren't they, Mummy?' She turned her smiling face up to Gemma's.

'They certainly are, poppet.' It was a golden opportunity. 'By the way, Dr Sam might call in later. He wants to talk to me about a patient he asked me to see this morning and the girl I went to see this afternoon. Sorry to bring shop talk home, love, but we've been so busy...'

'Oh, goody. I like Dr Sam. What's shop talk?'

CHAPTER SIX

SAM arrived promptly at eight. Gemma, trying to ignore the way her heartbeat quickened when the doorbell rang, marched firmly along the hall and flung wide the front door.

He was silhouetted against the red glow of the setting sun streaming across the green.

'Hi!' They both spoke simultaneously, breathily, then burst into laughter.

Sam, his eyes brimming with amusement, said, 'Shall we begin again?'

Gemma chuckled and the knot in her stomach dissolved. 'Good evening,' she said, bowing her head slightly in the manner of the gracious hostess. 'Please, do come in.'

'Thank you.' Grinning, he stepped into the small hall, towering over her.

Daisy came bounding out of the dining room, a bundle of energy in her jazzy pyjamas and huge fluffy slippers. 'Hello, Dr Sam. I'm ready for bed and I've had my bath, but I stay up till half past eight on Friday and Saturday nights as a treat.' She beamed him a dimpling smile. 'Would you like to see my homework? It's a drawing.'

Sam nodded and smiled down at her. 'I'd *love* to.' He accepted her hand, which she tucked confidently into his, and allowed himself to be led into the dining room.

'It's a picture of our house, but I haven't finished yet,' she explained as Sam bent over the table. She began pointing out the salient features, naming the various rooms behind the windows.

'And that's Mummy's room with the flowery curtains, but my room's not there, it's at the back and faces east and I've got blue curtains with birds and trees on.'

'What sort of birds?'

'Oh, robins and blackbirds and...'

Gemma stood just inside the door and surveyed the two bent heads so close together. Tendrils of Daisy's vibrant, red-bronze tresses seemed to reach out to touch Sam's thick, straight, corn-blond hair. She found herself holding her breath not wanting to disrupt the tableau. A curious sensation surged through her.

They looked so *right*, together—there was no other word to describe it. Like father and daughter, came the extraordinary thought.

She felt herself blushing and squashed the thought. She cleared her throat, but her voice still came out sounding husky.

'Would you like a drink, Sam? Coffee, wine?'

He lifted his head and smiled over his shoulder. 'Wine would be nice,' he said. 'A dry white if you have it.'

Was it her imagination at work again, or did *his* voice, too, sound huskier and deeper than usual? And had his smile a special quality about it?

'Right, coming up,' she murmured, as she drifted, feeling curiously detached, towards the kitchen.

The feeling of detachment and euphoria persisted as at Daisy's request the three of them played noisy games of Snap and Pairs Sam and Daisy each won games, with Gemma trailing a dismal third each time. She was accused by Daisy of not concentrating, and serenely agreed. Just as she found herself agreeing when Daisy's bedtime approached and, backed up by Sam, her happy little daughter begged to be allowed to stay up till nine o'clock.

Daisy, wide-eyed with astonishment, gave her a life-threatening hug, and then, to his pleased surprise, did the same to Sam.

By the time she was eventually settled for the night, and Gemma and Sam, calling a final cheerful goodnight, made their way downstairs, it was half past nine. It had been a strange, unreal experience for Gemma, finding herself sharing Daisy's bedtime ritual with anyone. A new experience for both of them, and Daisy had revelled in it.

Feeling thoroughly bemused, Gemma followed Sam down the stairs. She couldn't believe how easily she had been outwitted by her daughter who, out of the blue, had invited Sam to admire her newly decorated bedroom and had then cajoled him into reading a bedtime story.

'Sorry you got trapped into that,' she apologised stiffly, leading the way into the sitting room. She indicated an armchair. 'Please, sit down.' Suddenly, without Daisy's presence, she felt uptight and breathless. What had she let herself in for when she had agreed to him visiting, talking—what had they got to talk about? A look! Eye contact! A wordless exchange of vibes!

Sam grinned. 'Don't be. I'm a sucker for Thomas the Tank Engine, and it was a joy to read to Daisy—she's a darling.' And you're a darling too, he wanted to say. Beautiful, desirable, and I'd like to kiss your lovely mouth. Instead, he said softly, 'Relax, Gemma, love, I'm not going to pressure you. We're only going to talk.'

Love! What did he mean—*love*? He said that to patients, especially children whom he wanted to reassure. She herself said it to reassure. *She* didn't need reassuring. 'I *am* relaxed,' she insisted, trying to sound firm. She was let down by her voice, which came out a little squeaky.

He ignored the squeak, nodded and sat down. 'Do you think I might beg another glass of wine?'

She had just sat down in the opposite armchair, but catapulted to her feet. 'Oh, of course, I'll fetch the bottle from the fridge.' She bolted from the room.

In the kitchen, she stood motionless for a moment, taking deep breaths, fingers pressed against her hot cheeks. 'Get a hold of yourself, woman,' she muttered. 'You can handle the situation. It's no big deal.' Liar! OK, so it is a big deal. It's the biggest, maddest thing that's happened to you since Neil took off. This thing between you and Sam. But you're older and wiser, and forewarned is forearmed. All you have to do, Gemma Fellows, is to play it cool.

Play it cool! She snatched the ice-cold wine from the fridge and loaded it onto a tray with two glasses, added bowls of crisps and nuts and, keeping her back ramrod-straight, marched along the hall to the sitting room.

Sam was leaning back in his chair, his eyes closed, hands linked behind his head, long legs stretched out before him, feet crossed at the ankles. He was sound asleep.

Gemma stood, looking down at him. Her heart contracted. He looked totally at ease, younger and unexpectedly vulnerable, the tired lines round his mouth smoothed away.

Taking infinite care not to wake him, she placed the tray on the small round table between the chairs. But for all her care he heard her and his eyes flicked open to reveal brilliant chips of blue, immediately focused and alert.

'Good Lord,' he said, sitting up straight. 'Sorry about that. It's this room. It's charming, all these muted colours, gracious yet cosy. I'm afraid I dropped off.'

'Don't you think that the fact that you've only had a few hours' sleep over the last week, as well as working flat out during the day, might have something to do with it?' Gemma said drily. She felt good all at once, no longer tense and nervous but mature and practical, able to handle anything or anyone, even this charismatic man who threatened the defences she had long ago erected.

He grinned. 'Yep, you could be right. It has been a bit of a marathon, but that's to be expected in general practice, especially a virtually two-man one like ours.'

With a steady hand Gemma poured the wine and handed him a glass.

'Have you ever thought of taking on a third partner, not just relying on occasional help?' she asked.

Sam took a sip of wine. 'Dad and I have thought about it, but dismissed the idea. We're managing with Richard Thorn and Bob Carstairs, pro tem. They're both doctors we can trust to look after our patients the way we do and, believe me, doctors of that calibre are not thick on the ground.'

His eyes met Gemma's. The twinkle died out of them and they were suddenly bleak. 'That must sound incredibly conceited,' he said, his voice harsh, 'and we certainly haven't the monopoly on caring, but caring doctors seem to be few and far between these days. Some think you clock on at nine and off at five.'

'Tell me about it,' Gemma said bitterly. 'There are a lot of nurses who think like that too, especially in hospital. It's a techno-gadget-led career, with good old-fashioned TLC coming second best. And agency nurses being used instead of permanent staff. And un-trained people being given jobs to do that they shouldn't be, and all due to cuts and bad man-agement.'

She paused for a moment, then laughed un-certainly, and her eyes, which had glittered an-grily, softened.

'Sorry, rather a hobby-horse of mine. I can quite see why you and your father are reluctant to invite in another partner—you've such a unique set-up here. I never dreamed that I would be lucky enough to work in a place like this.' She lifted her glass in a sort of salute.

Sam leaned across and clinked his glass to hers. 'The luck is ours, Gemma. You fit in perfectly, this is where you belong—in Blaney St Mary.' His voice was like a caress, soft, warm, slightly husky, and his eyes suddenly full of tenderness.

Deep, sea blue eyes. I could drown in them, thought Gemma, and felt her lips forming the words to say it out loud. She drew in a sharp, painful breath and looked down into her drink. Oh, that would be just great! Pull yourself together, woman. You've been paid a compliment—think of something gracious to say.

She could find no words, gracious or otherwise. The seconds, perhaps minutes, ticked by. Painfully conscious of the steady tide of give-away red creeping into her cheeks, she said abruptly, 'By the way, Tracy Formby, little Gaz's mother, I went to see her...'

Her voice trailed off. It sounded like what it was, a totally artificial diversion. She could feel Sam's eyes focused on her face, and forced herself to look up and meet them, almost afraid of what she would find there.

The tender expression was still there, but laughter was there too. He'd seen through the diversion, but chose to go along with it.

'And how did the poor girl take the news about Gaz?' he asked, his voice calm and professional, every inch the concerned doctor.

Gemma gathered together her tattered wits. If he could be so professional, so could she. After all, she'd started this particular ball rolling.

She said evenly, 'Remarkably well. In fact, she didn't care a damn, or pretended not to. I'm not sure which. She seemed to hate the poor little chap. Her indifference, her abusiveness,shook me, though it shouldn't have done. I've heard it all before. And there's no reason why she shouldn't have come to the surgery. She isn't ill, at least...'

'At least?' Sam prompted.

'As far as I could make out, she hasn't got a temperature, hasn't vomited or had diarrhoea, which seems to put the current bug out of the picture. I just think she couldn't be bothered. But she's a bag of nerves, thin, chain smokes, looks as dirty and neglected as the baby.'

Sam frowned. 'Any sign she's doing drugs?'

'Not that I could see, but she was wearing a long-sleeved shirt and jeans so I couldn't see her legs or arms. And they're obviously church-mouse poor. I wouldn't have thought they could afford even the cheapest soft drug, never mind the hard stuff.'

'That's never stopped an addict before. And she smokes—that costs. I dare say she spends more on cigarettes than food. But you're probably right— She's not into drugs or she'd have been to the surgery for a fix on prescription.'.

His frown deepened. 'What a pathetic little family they are.'

Gemma looked across at him and felt the sudden sting of tears in her eyes. 'Pathetic's the word for it. I was *so* angry with her at first for neglecting the baby and not seeming to care.' Her voice wobbled. 'But thinking about it, talking about it…that horrible caravan… little Gaz… How *could* they manage? She's not much more than a child herself, and neither is Steve. At best, bringing up a baby is hard work. For them it must be hell. *Hell!* Oh, Sam.'

The held-back tears rolled down her cheeks. Suddenly Sam was there, drawing her up out of the chair, holding her in his arms, folding her against his chest. He nuzzled the top of her head. She could feel his warm breath stirring her hair. He tilted her head and kissed her forehead, her eyelids, her wet cheeks, and then her mouth, gently but firmly.

It was a long, lingering, loving kiss, a kiss to reassure, to let her know that he was there, would be there whenever she had need of him. At last he lifted his head and cupped her face with his long, narrow hands and wiped the last of her tears away with his thumbs.

His eyes smiled into hers. 'You needed that, love,' he said softly. 'We all need to cry sometimes. It's the best therapy, bar laughing.'

Gemma sniffed and he fished a clean handkerchief out of his pocket and held it to her nose. 'Have a good blow,' he said, a smile tilting the corners of his mouth.

She blew noisily into the large square of snowy-white cotton. 'Thanks.' She smiled up at him, a quivering smile, her mouth trembling with the effort. 'Sorry, shouldn't have broken down like that, very unprofessional.'

He pressed a forefinger to her lips. His brilliant eyes held hers.

'Unprofessional be damned. If anyone deserves to give way to a good howl, you do. In just over a couple of weeks you've moved house single-handed, started Daisy off at a new school and yourself off in a new demanding job. This afternoon's episode with little Gaz just acted as a catalyst. Brought back memories of the struggle you had to bring up Daisy on your own. I'm right, Gemma, aren't I?'

She nodded.

He stroked her cheek. 'And you had Miss Heinman to cope with last weekend, *and* for good measure you've decorated Daisy's room. Good Lord, woman, you must be exhausted.'

'Yes, I think I am a bit tired,' she admitted, feeling suddenly intensely weary.

Sam smoothed her hair back from her face and kissed the corners of her drooping mouth.

'Bath and bed,' he said, turning her round to face the door.

'But…' She waved her hand over the table with the empty glasses and bowls of nuts and crisps.

'No problem. I'll tidy up and see myself out.'

With his hands on her shoulders, he steered her to the bottom of the stairs. 'Up you go, love.'

He gave her a gentle shove and she slowly mounted the first few steps. She was halfway up when he said softly, 'What are you doing tomorrow, Gemma?'

She paused and looked down at him over her shoulder. 'We're going to Shillingbourne, shopping and swimming, in the morning.'

'No plans for the afternoon?'

'Depends on the weather. If it's fine we thought we might climb up Round Hill—they say the view from the top is fantastic.'

'We used to call it Kite Hill when we were kids. Has Daisy got a kite?'

'No.'

'If I supply a kite, may I join you, or is this a strictly mother-and-daughter outing?'

Gemma's pulse rate doubled. She shook her head. 'Not at all, the more the merrier.'

'About twoish?'

'Fine.'

By midway through Monday morning, the weekend was for Gemma but a dream, as work took over with a vengeance. But between patients memories of it kept flitting into her mind. She could almost *feel* the wind lifting her hair as she and Sam and Daisy stood on the top of Round Hill on Saturday afternoon.

Ruthlessly squashing the vivid picture of an ecstatic Daisy, guided by a laughing Sam, controlling the soaring, swooping kite sailing high above their heads, she went out to the waiting room to call in her umpteenth patient, a Mrs Gloria Watson.

Mrs Watson was a cheerful, heavily pregnant lady in her late thirties. She was wearing large, sloppy men's trainers with a neat maternity trouser suit.

She beamed at Gemma as she limped over to a chair and sat down. 'Thanks for squeezing me in, Nurse,' she said. 'I don't want to worry either of the doctors if it's not necessary. I hope you'll be able to help me. Ellie says you're brilliant.'

'Competent, rather,' said Gemma with a laugh. 'But I warn you, I'm a bit rusty on my midwifery.'

'Oh, it's nothing to do with this.' Mrs Watson patted her bulging tummy. 'That's fine. It's my big toe. I stubbed it last night, tripped up a step. It bled quite a bit and hurt like mad. The nail was a bit wobbly so I put an Elastoplast on it, but it's stuck and bled a lot when I tried to remove it this morning. That's why I'm wearing my husband's trainers—they're more comfortable than any of my shoes.'

'I did wonder,' said Gemma. She placed a stool under the injured foot. 'Right, let's have a look at your poor old toe.'

The toe was a mess, oozing blood and pus, the nail half hanging off. Gemma cleaned it up with antiseptic, applied an anaesthetiser, and with infinite care removed the shattered nail where it was still attached to the damaged nail bed. The area round the toe was swollen and bruised.

Mrs Watson hissed in a couple of sharp breaths, but otherwise maintained a stoic silence.

'Well done.' Gently Gemma swabbed the exposed raw flesh with more antiseptic. 'Having a nail removed is a painful business.' She ran her fingers lightly over the big toe joint and smaller bones adjoining it. 'And I think you may have broken a bone or two as well as ripping your nail off. I'll have to get one of the doctors to check it to see if it needs to be X-rayed. And you need an antibiotic to counter the infection. I'm just going to cover it with gauze until one of them can take a look at it.'

It was a smiling Sam who breezed in a few minutes later in response to her phone call to Ellie. Gemma returned his smile and her heart fluttered like a cloud of butterflies in her chest—she hadn't seen him since Saturday.

He crouched down in front of the patient and whistled softly between his teeth when he saw the injured toe. He sat back on his heels. 'I'm afraid you'll have to go into Shillingbourne Cottage for an X-ray, Gloria, to establish whether you've broken anything. Meanwhile…' he quirked a quizzical sideways glance up at Gemma, one eyebrow raised a fraction higher than the other '…I think a Kaltostat dressing to clean up that pus and a small padded splint to keep the toe in alignment, don't you, Nurse?'

His eyes glinted, her heart thudded. She nodded. 'Fine.' Her voice came out as a throaty murmur, and she repeated loudly. 'Fine.'

A hank of hair fell across Sam's forehead and she had to resist the sudden desire to smooth it back in place. What on earth? Her cheeks burned and she busied herself disposing of the dirty implements and bowls on the trolley, fervently hoping that he hadn't noticed anything amiss.

He stood up and smiled down at Gloria. 'I'll get in touch with the hospital right now. See

Ellie on your way out—she'll tell you when to go for your X-ray, which should be later today. And I'll leave your prescription for an antibiotic with her.'

He paused at the door. 'And promise me you won't try to drive yourself into Shillingbourne. I know you think you're tough as old boots, but that just wouldn't be on.'

Gloria grinned. 'OK, promise. Mum'll take me if Phil's working. She insisted on bringing me in this morning. She's outside in the waiting room.'

'Sensible woman, your mum,' said Sam, and with a nod and a smile for both of them he took himself off.

'If I weren't happily spoken for,' sighed Gloria, 'I'd go for our Dr Sam in a big way. He wouldn't know what hit him. Of course, I've known him since for ever. He used to be quite a lad, played the field. I heard that he nearly got caught once, but wriggled off the hook.' She sighed again. 'But he's gorgeous, isn't he, Nurse?'

You can say that again, thought Gemma. 'He's very nice,' she mumbled as she bent over the injured foot. What did that mean—wriggled off the hook? With practised fingers, she fixed the dressing and the splint in place with a firm supporting bandage. 'I'm afraid you won't be able to get your trainer on,' she explained, when she'd finished bandaging from toe to ankle, gently easing the thick sock over the bulky dressing.

'Not to worry,' replied Gloria cheerfully, and with Gemma's support hobbled out to the waiting room to join her mother.

There were four more patients for Gemma to see before lunch. Working on autopilot and concentrating fiercely, she dealt with them with her usual calm so that none of them guessed at the turmoil she was in. But it was a relief when the session ended and she could get ready to go home for lunch to think. She had to get herself straightened out.

She had nearly made a fool of herself in front of a patient. Supposing she had pushed back that lock of Sam's hair… It didn't bear thinking about. It was ridiculous at her age— frightening to think that she had so nearly given herself away. What on earth was happening to her?

Ellie called to her as she was letting herself out of the staff door, wanting to know if she would be back early for coffee. Gemma had decided to skip that ritual for once, but couldn't refuse the pleading tone in Ellie's voice, and confirmed that she would.

She tried to make sense of what was happening to her and Sam as she nibbled at a sandwich a few minutes later. What was it between them? Simply chemistry, all body scents and hormones? Lust rather than love? And was it affecting him as strongly as it was her? Did she invade *his* mind as he did hers?

He'd been so gentle and kind on Friday evening when he'd mopped up her tears and comforted her. It had been exactly what she'd needed then, but if…*if* this seemingly mutual attraction was going anywhere, she would want more than avuncular comfort from him, a replacement father for Daisy. She would want companionship, laughter, sex and promises of something more to come…

The thought stopped her in her tracks. What the devil was she doing, even thinking along those lines? Dear God, she hardly knew the man and here she was making some sort of future plans round him—and all on the strength of eye contact and body language and one real kiss. That farewell kiss on Saturday had been something! There had been nothing avuncular about *that*.

Altogether, Saturday had been brilliant: Kite-flying on the hill; a farmhouse tea in a village in the valley the other side; walking back home with a tired Daisy riding high on Sam's shoulders. It had been a happy family outing.

What else could it have been, since it had been largely devoted to entertaining Daisy? But, then, for years her weekends had been devoted to Daisy and, being the sort of man he was, Sam had sussed that out for himself.

The easy companionship had continued after Daisy had gone to bed. They had watched a film and had held a post-mortem on it as they'd consumed the bottle of wine Sam had brought with him. She had accused him laughingly of trying to get her tipsy.

He had gone along with the cliché. 'What, so that I might have my wicked way with you?' he'd said with a leer, his blue eyes blazing. They had even flirted a little, keeping it light, veering away from anything serious— until he had kissed her goodnight. That had been anything but lightweight.

Standing in the hall just inside the front door, Sam said with sudden deadly seriousness, looking into her eyes with an intensity that was almost frightening, 'Is there any reason why I shouldn't kiss you as I want to kiss you, as you deserve to be kissed, Gemma?'

There was Daisy, and a dozen other reasons—most of them to do with the fact that no man had figured seriously in her life since she'd parted from Neil. The barricade she had erected then had remained intact.

'No,' she whispered.

'Your ex?'

'Is very ex.'

'Positive?'

'Positive!' She *was* positive.

'And there's no one else?'

'No one.'

He bent his head and his mouth closed over hers, at first tenderly then savagely, and she had responded like a flower in the desert thirsting for rain. Their bodies had melded, soft breasts crushed painfully to hard chest; hip to hip, thigh gyrated against thigh, rousing, exciting; tongues explored, teeth nibbled lips.

Sam gave a groan. His hands, which had been cupping her buttocks, crept up her back and slid up into the thick bob of her hair. He tilted back her head and rubbed his nose to hers. 'Oh, Gemma, I don't know what you've done to me,' he murmured thickly, 'but you've made your way deep under my skin.'

The murmured words had come like manna from heaven—under his skin, that's just where she wanted to be. Gemma shivered, her heart hammered as if it would bound from her chest—but suddenly out of the blue warning bells rang in her head. This isn't right, it's too soon, they seemed to clamour. She eased herself away from him, gently but firmly. 'I think you'd better go,' she said, her voice quaking.

His intelligent eyes gazed steadily down into hers. 'You want more time.' It was a statement not a question.

'Yes.'

'You have it, love.' His voice was gentle. 'Just think about it. See you at the surgery on Monday.' And turning on his heel, he let himself out of the front door.

Think about it. She'd done precious little else but think about it since then. The memory of that kiss and its implication had been with her all through Sunday. Somehow she had survived the day without rousing Daisy's suspicions.

It had helped that they went to tea with her best friend, Katy. While the two girls had played together, Gemma and Katy's mother, Mary, had chatted about this and that and laid the foundation for future friendship. But that had been Sunday—today's revelation by Gloria Watson about Sam's youthful past, especially the bit about him sliding off the hook, was a whole new ball game. It had suggested that he had backed off from commitment. Neil had been good at backing off from commitment. Or was there another explanation?

The chiming of the grandfather clock jerked Gemma back to the present, reminding her that it was time she returned to the surgery and her chat with Ellie.

Ellie had barely got started on a résumé of her disastrous weekend with her in-laws when the patients' doorbell pealed several times in quick succession.

They abandoned their coffee and made for the door.

'Somebody sounds frantic,' said Gemma, as Ellie punched in the security sequence to release the outer and inner doors.

An elderly man, grey in the face, stood on the doorstep. He was shaking badly and clutching the left side of his chest. 'Pain,' he said. 'Terrible pain.' He sagged against the doorframe. Gemma and Ellie caught him as he slid towards the ground.

'Know him?' asked Gemma, as between them they half carried him, his feet dragging, into the waiting room.

'No, I'm sure he's not one of ours. There was a car parked at a crazy angle to the kerb— must be his. Is he having a heart attack?' puffed Ellie as they laid the man gently down on the floor.

'Possibly.' Gemma was taking the man's pulse at his wrist. It was weak and uneven. 'Loosen his tie, Ellie, and fetch the mobile oxygen pack and a blanket, then get hold of Sam or his father, or both. We're going to have to carry him to the treatment room.'

Both doctors came within minutes, and the four of them carried the man to the treatment room. Breathing raggedly through the oxygen mask, he came round as they lowered him onto the couch. He stared blearily up at the strange faces and frowned and fumbled at the mask.

Sam bent over him. 'Best keep it on, old chap,' he said, plugging his stethoscope into his ears as Gemma unbuttoned the man's shirt. 'I'm a doctor. You're in the Blaney St Mary surgery.'

The sound of voices filtered through from the waiting room.

'Doesn't look like he's going to arrest,' murmured Dr Mallory, 'but he's going to have to be hospitalised. Sam, you and Gemma carry on here, Ellie will phone for an ambulance and then between us we'll sort out the invading hordes—OK by you?'

'Fine.' Sam nodded and began his examination. A few minutes later he straightened up. 'I think you've had a mild heart attack,' he told the elderly man gently. 'Have you had any heart trouble before, Mr...?'

'Blake.' The colourless lips trembled. 'No, I haven't. Is it serious, Doctor?' He put out a shaky hand.

Sam took it and gave him a reassuring smile. 'All heart attacks are serious and have to be followed up, Mr Blake, but yours is a mild one, a warning to take care. Now, I'm going to give you something for the pain and arrange for you to go into hospital for tests. Is there anyone we can notify?'

He gave the name of his daughter who lived in London, and gave her telephone number. Gemma made a note of it as he reeled it off. He was a widower, holidaying in Shillingbourne. Would they let the hotel manager know? He was worried about his car. He was agitated, worried about everything.

Sam gave him a painkilling injection and a mild sedative to calm him down. He and Gemma both assured him that they would take care of everything. They stayed with him, monitoring his heart, blood pressure, pulse and respirations until the ambulance arrived twenty minutes later. They saw him into the ambulance, then, standing side by side on the gravel strip outside the surgery, waited until it had departed and their patient was safely away.

Their hands were almost touching. Gemma felt the hairs on her bare forearms stir. He had his shirtsleeves rolled up and she could feel the warmth radiating from his skin, was aware of the curling fair hairs on *his* arms, glinting in the sunshine. Her cheeks flushed, she glanced sideways at him. 'I must get on, I'm miles behind with my list.'

His fingers closed over hers. 'Don't go.' His voice was low, urgent. 'Another minute's not going to make any difference.' He squeezed her hand tightly. 'Gemma, about Saturday, can we…?'

His voice was drowned out as a red sports car roared round the green and screeched to a halt at the kerbside in front of them. He stared. The car looked familiar. Of course it was. He'd seen it outside Cherry Tree Cottage the Sunday before last when he'd witnessed that strange little tableau…

'Bloody hell!' He looked at Gemma. He couldn't read the expression on her face. 'Do you know this maniac?' he asked.

She nodded. 'Yes,' she hissed through clenched teeth. 'I do. It's Neil, my ex-husband.'

CHAPTER SEVEN

AN INCREDULOUS expression swept over Sam's face. 'So this the husband who is supposed to be *very ex*,' he ground out. Dropping Gemma's hand as if it were on fire, he turned and disappeared through the surgery door.

Gemma stood like a statue staring after him. What did he mean—'very ex', in that sarcastic tone? And what was Neil doing here? And why, oh *why* had he come when she and Sam—?

'Surprise, surprise, Gem, darling.' She turned back to see him bounding across toward her, a boyish, exuberant smile on his face, doing his Peter Pan act.

He skidded to a halt in front of her, scuffing up the gravel. Just like a small child, she thought crossly.

'Hello, sweetie, long time no see.' He bent his head as if to kiss her. She stepped smartly back.

Sweetie! She hated him calling her sweetie, always had. It grated. She wasn't dead keen on

Gem either—it was what he used to call her. She'd loved it then when they were young and in love, but now... She didn't want to think about that.

'Rubbish, Neil, you were here just over a week ago, and I told you then about coming without phoning first. Right now Daisy's at school and I'm working so I suggest you take yourself off somewhere and come to the cottage at four o'clock when we'll both be home.'

Give me time to prepare Daisy, she thought—and with the thought a wave of sadness that she had to be prepared for a visit from her father.

Neil's full lips—too full—turned down at the corners. So different from Sam's finely sculpted lips, sprang another thought. 'Couldn't you hook her out of school early?'

'No, and, anyway, I'm working. See you at four at the cottage.' Turning on her heel, she let herself into the surgery.

Ellie looked surprised to see her. 'Sam said you'd got a visitor and might be a while and suggested I might change some of your appointments,' she said.

'Did he now?' Gemma produced a tight smile. 'No need. As you see, I'm here. But be a love and phone the school, please, and tell them that if I'm late collecting Daisy...' She hesitated. Neil wouldn't, would he, take her out in that lethal car of his? 'They're not to let her go with anyone else.'

Ellie looked at her, her eyes popping with curiosity.

Not surprising, thought Gemma. It must sound a bit cloak and daggerish. 'I know it sounds odd, I'll explain tomorrow, but don't say anything to anyone else, Ellie, please?'

Ellie shook her head. 'Not if you don't want me to.'

'Thanks.' Gemma smiled an apology to a couple of patients waiting behind her and fled to the treatment room.

She crushed thoughts of both Sam and Neil out of her mind and got on with her list. As Ellie had warned, there were a number of people wanting jabs before going on holiday or hay-fever sufferers needing antihistamines, in addition to the normal chores.

She was surprised to find that a number of those wanting holiday jabs were off to some far-flung places. She found herself administering vaccines against a range of diseases from cholera to typhoid. This had been the norm when she was nursing in the London practice, but unexpected in rural Blaney St Mary—at least, she thought with a snort of self-disgust, to a townee like me. Why, because someone lives in the country and speaks with a thick local burr, should they be content with the Costa Brava? How patronising could you get?

The list went without a hitch until Jo Pullen and his wife came in for first-time jabs. They were off to Saudi Arabia. Jo Pullen was a heavily built, middle-aged man who nearly fainted at the sight of the needle. He had to be persuaded by Gemma, and jollied along by an exasperated Mrs Pullen, that he would feel little more than a scratch before he would even roll up his shirtsleeve.

'So you say,' he said grimly, squeezing his eyes shut as Gemma swabbed his arm and bent over him with the syringe. 'But I can't abide needles, that's why I don't like going further afield than Brittany—that suits me fine.'

'All done,' said Gemma seconds later, putting a tiny dressing over the minute puncture mark.

Mr Pullen opened his eyes cautiously. 'You mean, you've finished?' he asked. 'But I didn't feel a thing. You're a wizard, Nurse.'

'If you say so, Mr Pullen,' replied Gemma, smiling at him and his wife. 'So tell me, why are you going to Saudi Arabia this year instead of Brittany?'

Mrs Pullen answered. 'We're going to see our son. He works in Saudi and is treating us to this holiday. I'm looking forward to it. It'll make a nice change, and it'll be lovely to see him and his family.'

'All sand and flies, I dare say,' grumbled Mr Pullen, but he smiled. He tapped his arm and rolled down his sleeve. 'But at least the worst is over, thanks to you, Nurse.'

Gemma saw them out and called for her next and last patient—Mrs Janice Norton—for removal of stitches from a hand wound, she saw from her notes.

Janice had a tiny baby secured to her chest in a front sling and was struggling with a reluctant, grizzly small boy of about three with her one good hand, the other hand being bandaged.

Gemma went to meet her. 'Let me help,' she offered, and, gently but firmly detaching the boy from his mother, led the way to the treatment room.

Surprised, the boy stopped grizzling and stared up at Gemma. She smiled. 'My name's Gemma,' she said as she sat him down on the spare chair. 'What's your name, love?'

He stuck his thumb in his mouth and continued to stare.

'It's Adam, Nurse.' supplied his mother. 'He's a bit shy with strangers.'

'He'll grow out of it,' Gemma said, handing Adam a picture book which he took with one hand whilst keeping his thumb plugged into his mouth. 'Is he at playschool yet?'

Janice said wryly, 'You've got to be joking. The nearest one's in Shillingbourne, and it's expensive. No way could we afford it. But he's already booked in for the reception class at the school—he can go there when he's four.'

'Oh, well, not to worry, he'll soon have his...brother, or is it sister...?'

'Sister.'

'To play with,' Gemma said cheerfully. She stroked the sleeping baby's soft cheek. 'Now, let's have a look at this hand of yours, Janice, see if the stitches are ready to come out.'

She unwound the bandage and removed the dressing that had been applied over the diagonal wound. 'It's looking good, coming to-

gether well. Dr Sam did a neat bit of stitching.
I'll remove most of them, but one or two will
have to stay in for another couple of days.' She
glanced at the young mother. 'I dare say
you've been using it more than you should—
yes?'

Janice shrugged. 'Can't help it with these
two to see to.' She dropped a kiss on her
baby's head and smiled across at Adam, still
sucking his thumb but absorbed in the book.
'Especially as Adam's a bit mummy-sick at
present.'

Deftly, Gemma began removing the
stitches—sibling jealousy? she wondered. 'Do
you let Adam help you with the baby?' she
asked, keeping her voice low. 'Let him hold
her sometimes, help when she has a bath?'

'Oh, I wouldn't dare. He's clumsy, he
doesn't seem to realise that Tansy needs to be
handled with care.'

Poor Adam! There was no doubt that he was
loved, but… Gemma finished removing all but
three stitches, swabbed the palm with antiseptic and applied a small, waterproof dressing to
the healing area.

'Come back and see me in three days and
I'll take out those last few stitches,' she said.

She sat back in her chair. Now comes the tricky bit, she thought. This poor woman's anxious and unhappy. I must try and help. Still keeping her voice low, she said, 'Why don't you explain to Adam that because Tansy is small she has to be treated gently, like he was when he was a baby. Sit him down somewhere safe and show him how to hold her, ask him to help you push the pram—anything to make him feel involved. And try to give him a little time on his own and throw in lots of hugs and kisses.'

Janice frowned. 'I haven't been neglecting him, if that's what you think.' She sounded indignant. 'But there's so much to do, and my husband comes in at all hours, wanting a meal. I just get so tired.'

Wanting or demanding? 'Janice, it's crystal clear that you haven't been neglecting Adam, that you love him to bits, but make sure that *he* knows that. The baby inevitably takes up so much of your time that he may be feeling a bit left out. Perhaps your husband could—'

'*No!*' An explosive no. 'He's too busy and...to tell you the truth, Nurse, he isn't too keen on the kids.' Her voice dropped to a whisper. 'He didn't want to have children. I think he's a bit jealous of them.' She crossed over to Adam and removed the book from his hand. 'Come on, love.' she said huskily, helping him down from the chair. 'Let's go home to tea and watch something on the telly.'

My word, thought Gemma, have I said too much or too little?

Janice paused at the door. 'Thanks, Nurse, I'll remember what you've said, it makes sense. I don't know why I hadn't realised what was happening.' She pulled a face. 'I must be thick, but things will be different from now on.'

'You're tired, not thick, Janice. Why don't you make an appointment to see Dr Sam? Your hormones may be all over the place— they often are when you've had a baby. If it is that, he might be able to prescribe something to sort them out.'

The young mother's face lit up. 'It would be brilliant just not to feel so exhausted. I'll make an appointment right now. Thanks again, Nurse, you're a gem.'

A gem! How ironic. Thoughtfully, Gemma tidied the treatment room, disposing of dirty dressings and wiping down surfaces. Had she been too optimistic with Janice, suggesting that Sam might come up with a miracle pill to cure her postnatal exhaustion? No, it had been the right thing to do. Even if he didn't produce a magic pill, he would listen, offer guidance and show that he cared. To someone like Janice, who seemed to be starved of caring—certainly by her husband—that could work like magic.

Sam! Just saying his name in her head, it did strange things to her heart, making it leap about inside her chest like a wild thing. She sat down hard on a chair. This was ridiculous. She shouldn't feel like this, especially after the way he'd walked away from her with that caustic remark when Neil arrived.

Oh, God. Neil. She looked at her watch. A quarter past three. She'd have to scoot if she was to have time to explain his arrival to Daisy.

Daisy was subdued when Neil arrived, returning his noisy kiss with a cautious one of her own. But she smiled, if a little hesitantly, when, with a flourish, he produced a large, oblong, beautifully wrapped package and handed it to her.

'There you are, poppet, to remind you of how much Daddy loves you.'

'Thank you, Daddy.' Her voice was trembly with excitement, her round face rosy as she laid the parcel on the table and knelt up on a chair to open it. Her nimble fingers made short work of removing the outer wrappings.

Gemma tried not to mind her eagerness, her ready acceptance of the present from the father whom she half distrusted. She's only six, Gemma reminded herself, it's only natural. But, oh, please, my darling, she prayed silently, don't be fooled by him. He's still the same irresponsible man who walked out on us, couldn't handle being a father. Expensive presents can't alter that.

It *was* an expensive present—an angelic-faced, elegantly dressed doll in pink satin, a walking, talking, laughing, crying, singing doll.

For a moment, speechless, Daisy stared at it, stroked its rose-tinted cheek with a chubby forefinger, then lifted it reverently from its silk-lined box and cuddled it close.

Her green eyes sparkled. 'Oh, Mummy, isn't she beautiful?' she breathed.

'Beautiful,' Gemma agreed, pumping enthusiasm into her voice. She touched the gold-tinted curls. It was a little girl's dream doll.

God knew how much it had cost. For once she envied Neil, or rather envied the fact that he could afford to buy a present for their daughter that brought such a glow to her dear little face.

Not, she reminded herself, that Daisy glowed like that only for expensive presents. She would do the same for much simpler things, like a book or paints or crayons. She was an unspoilt, easy-to-please child, but there was no doubt that the doll had hit a high spot. And why not? For once Neil had got it right. Be generous to him.

She ruffled Daisy's hair. 'You're a lucky girl,' she said. 'Don't you think that Daddy deserves a thank-you kiss?'

Daisy leaned across the corner of the table and kissed his cheek. 'Thank you, Daddy, for my beautiful, beautiful doll.'

'What about this one, then?' said Neil, offering his other cheek.

Daisy kissed it quickly, then scrambled back onto her chair.

'I could do with a hug too,' he said. 'Come here, poppet.'

A small frown creased Daisy's forehead, but she slid off the chair and, cuddling the doll, walked round the table.

Oh, Neil, don't push it, Gemma prayed. Don't make a big deal out of it. Just give her a quick hug and let her go.

He didn't hear her prayer or, if he did, ignored it, pulling Daisy roughly onto his lap and demanding another kiss as well as a hug. So what was new? He never had been sensitive to her thoughts or the vibes she had sent out to him in those early days of their marriage when she had still loved him. But be fair, she told herself. Not many men are intuitive or perceptive. You've got to spell everything out for them.

Sam is, murmured an inner voice. Is he? So why did he march away from me this afternoon? Why didn't he *see* that I was upset by Neil's arrival instead of—?

'Daddy, please, let me go. You're hugging me too tight and you're hurting my dolly.' Daisy's voice shattered her thoughts.

'*Neil!*' Gemma said sharply. 'Let Daisy get down—*now*.'

'Jealous.' He leered at her, grinning.

'No, but she's thanked you. Don't spoil it. Let her go, you're frightening her.' She put steel in her voice. 'I mean it Neil.'

Neil loosed his hold a little and looked down at Daisy. 'I don't frighten you, do I, poppet?'

Wide-eyed, Daisy stared up at him. She shook her head slightly. 'But I want to get down, please, and so does...Rose. She wants to get down, too.'

His mouth went sulky. 'Oh, well, if that's what you want.' He almost pushed her off his lap.

Clutching her doll, Daisy stood for a moment looking uncertainly from her father to her mother. A tug-of-war kid, thought Gemma, her heart going out to her small daughter.

She said softly, 'Listen, love, why don't you go and phone your friend Katy and tell her all about...Rose? Use the phone in my room.' She looked hard at Neil, willing him not to say or do anything to upset Daisy further. 'Katy,' she explained, 'is Daisy's best friend at school.'

Daisy's eyes were shining as she sidled towards the door to the hall. 'Oh, Mummy, can I? That's brilliant.' She whisked out through the door, banging it closed behind her.

Silence descended like a blanket as Gemma and Neil stared at each other across the table.

Ignore what's happened, Gemma told herself. Be pleasant, sociable. 'Would you like something to drink?' she asked. 'Coffee, tea?'

Still looking sulky, he grunted. 'Got anything stronger?'

'I thought as you were driving...' She hadn't thought anything of the sort—she'd known he'd want something stronger.

'Wine—red, white?' Deliberately she didn't mention the half-bottles of gin and whisky, survivors from her farewell party when she'd left London.

'Well, if that's all you've got... Red... please.' Suddenly the boyish smile was back. 'Nice to know you still care, Gem, about me drinking and driving. Don't want me to have an accident.'

'I don't want *anyone* to have an accident, especially one that can be avoided,' she said repressively. 'I saw what drinking and driving could do when I worked in Casualty.' She made for the door. 'I won't be a moment, the wine's in the kitchen.'

He was standing at the window, staring out across the green, when she came back. She crossed the room and stood beside him, handing him a glass.

'Cheers.' He clinked his glass to hers.

'Cheers.' She couldn't think of anything else to say, just longed for him to be gone. The thought brought a lump to her throat. She had loved him once…so much. If only, if only…

He knocked back the wine in one long swallow, then looked at his watch. 'Damn, have to be off, though I wish I could stay…' He gave Gemma a long considering look, and before she could move he planted a wet kiss on her mouth. 'You know, Gem, we should get back together again, you and I.'

Speechless, Gemma gaped at him for a moment, then found her voice. 'And Daisy?' she asked drily.

He shrugged. 'Of course, Daisy. Goes without saying.'

The tenderness of her thoughts a moment ago seeped away. 'That's big of you.'

He ignored, or didn't notice, her sarcasm. 'So, what about it Gem? Shall we give it a go?'

Gemma drew in a deep, deep breath that came from way beneath her diaphragm. 'I think if anything had better go Neil, it had better be you, right now.'

He looked at her, no, leered at her, and said, sounding almost triumphant, 'Afraid of falling for me again, Gem, or haven't you got over the first time?'

Gemma stared at him in disbelief. Of course she'd got over him. Did he really imagine that she could still love him after the way he'd deserted her, leaving her with a baby, knowing that her parents were living abroad? That she'd been on her own? His conceit was breathtaking, but, then, that was all part of the little boy act.

Extraordinary that he was such a whiz kid in the business world. Probably much of that was due to his charm, and he had oodles of that—and knew how to use it. Thank God, she was now immune to his charm.

She removed the empty glass from his hand and said blandly, 'The first time was the last time, Neil. Now it's time you were off. You've got a dinner date.'

'Yes, but I'll be back…soon.'

Please, not soon. 'Next time, please, phone.'

They moved out into the hall. He looked up the stairs.

'I'll say goodbye to Daisy for you,' Gemma said, making her voice casual, hoping he wouldn't insist on saying goodbye himself. Daisy, she thought, had had just about enough of her father for one day, and *she'd* certainly had enough of her ex-husband.

A few minutes later, with a sigh of relief, she watched as he noisily revved up the engine and drove away.

Gemma lay awake much of the night going over the events of the day, and rose feeling ragged.

Neil's suggestion that they get back together made her furious, and a touch scared, though she wasn't quite sure why. He wouldn't deliberately physically harm her or Daisy, but he was given to little boy tantrums when he couldn't get his own way, which was disconcerting to say the least.

As for Sam's curtness, that still hurt and made her heart ache. *Why* had he acted so out of character, so rudely? What had he read into Neil's arrival? What had made him suddenly turn to ice when only minutes before they had been working side by side on the elderly Mr

Pullen? She would tackle him about it at the first opportunity.

She worried, too, about Daisy, and her reaction to her father's visit. Silly, really, she told herself, as Daisy had gone happily to bed with Rose lying in state beside her, seemingly having forgotten being over-hugged by Neil. As if to confirm this, Daisy bounced into her room minutes later, her usual happy, chatty self, carrying Rose with exaggerated care. The episode was clearly forgotten.

The church clock struck a quarter to nine as Gemma made her way across the green to the surgery. Perhaps, she thought, like Daisy, Sam and I can forget yesterday's incident. She smiled wryly. Who are you kidding? she mused as she let herself in through the staff door. He'll probably avoid me like the plague and won't give me a chance to ask why he'd reacted as he had.

As it happened, fate decided that even if he'd wanted to, he couldn't ignore her. His corn-bright head bent in his usual solicitous manner, he was giving an arm to an elderly lady leaving his office. He looked up as Gemma closed and locked the staff door.

'Morning.' His voice was clipped.

Gemma's heart turned over several times. 'Morning,' she replied, mustering a smile and a nod that included the patient.

The tightest of smiles touched Sam's lips. She was near enough to see that it didn't reach his eyes. They were unreadable, the laughter lines radiating from them just lines. Maybe he was simply tired, he'd been on call last night.

In a toneless voice he asked. 'May I have a word, Nurse, please, if you can spare a moment, in my office in, say, five minutes?'

Gemma beamed, though her heart thudded into her shoes. He sounded so stiff, formal, unfriendly. 'Fine. I'll be there, Doctor.'

She let herself into the staffroom. She shrugged herself out of her jacket, ran a comb through her long bob of hair and stared in the mirror. Jade green eyes stared back at her, thoughtful, puzzled—*sad!* Why sad? Because Sam…because Sam's bitterly angry with you, she told her reflection, and that hurts. Angry! With little reason, she reminded herself sharply. For heaven's sake, where's your spunk, woman? You're the one who has a right to be angry. He's the one who walked away.

OK, supposing he was angry because Neil had arrived, driving dangerously like a bat out of hell. Surely that wasn't enough to ignore him the way he had or to humiliate her. It was almost as if he had a personal motive for refusing to stay to be introduced. But that wasn't possible. He not only didn't know Neil, he didn't know anything about him. She'd hardly mentioned him, except to acknowledge him as her ex-husband.

Ex-husband, that's what seemed to be bugging him. No, not ex, but *very ex*. He'd said it when he'd turned on his heel, almost as if he didn't believe it. Did he think that because she and Neil were divorced he shouldn't come anywhere near her? Surely he appreciated that ex-husband didn't mean ex-father, and that for Daisy's sake he was entitled to visit.

Or did he think…could he possibly think that Neil still held a place in her affections? Was that what the sarcasm had been about?

Did he resent it, loathe it, because he felt he had a *right* to? She almost stopped breathing for a moment as the thought sunk in, swirled around in her head… OK, they were mutually attracted—no, more than that, his kiss had said more than that the other night.

Five minutes, he'd said—five minutes had passed. Her chest full of butterflies, she made her way slowly to Sam's office. She tried to marshal her muddled thoughts, but they refused to be marshalled, and she found herself just as muddled when she knocked on his door and entered in response to his invitation.

His back to the door, he was silhouetted against the window looking over the walled orchard and twisted chimneys of the manor house. Gemma stood just inside the door, tense and expectant, waiting for him to speak.

After what seemed an eternity he turned round. Against the light she couldn't see his face clearly, or the expression in his eyes.

He said abruptly, 'I must apologise for the way I behaved yesterday. I shouldn't have walked away from you as I did. I should have waited to be introduced to...' he hesitated '...your husband.'

His voice was colourless. Gemma felt as if her heart were being squeezed by an ice-cold hand.

'Ex-husband.'

Sam took a step forward. She could see his face now. He was frowning, his mouth a firm line, his eyes were so dark they were almost navy blue.

'Are you sure he's really ex?' His voice had hardened. Where was the kind, caring doctor, the kind, caring man, the man of perception?

Gemma felt a mixture of disbelief, anger and intense sadness surging through her. She had thought that this man knew her—and she knew him—but...

'I said ex the other night, and I meant it. Why don't you believe me?' Her voice came out in a vaporous whisper. Her lips felt white, it was painful to speak. She felt her eyes glistening with held back tears. She clenched her teeth—*no way* would she cry. For heaven's sake, there was nothing to cry about—he was simply a man like any other man.

Sam took another step forward, his eyes searching her face. He punched one fist into the other. 'Shi—' He bit off the word. He reached out a tentative hand and touched her shoulder. 'Gemma, I don't know how to cope with this...this jealousy.'

Jealousy! All the thoughts in her mind tumbled together. '*Jealousy*,' she repeated incredulously. Incongruously she remembered that

Neil had accused her of jealousy when he'd cuddled Daisy.

'That's right, good old-fashioned jealousy...' The internal telephone on his desk sprang into life. He muttered under his breath as he turned and snatched up the receiver. 'Yes?' he barked, then said more quietly, 'Sorry, Ellie, what can I do for you?'

Gemma stared at the back of Sam's bright head, her tumultuous thoughts spiralling. *Jealousy!* There was an old song about jealousy... The murmur of Ellie's voice penetrated her thoughts. She caught the words 'came off his bike' and 'grazed legs'. An accident... Making a conscious effort, she snapped into professional mode.

Sam was saying, 'Can he walk? Good. Gemma's here. We'll come through and take him to the treatment room. Anyone with him? No? Then you'd better let his mum know, Ellie.'

He put down the phone and turned back to face Gemma. His lips were curled in a lopsided, sardonic smile. 'Sorry about that, might have known it would happen. Another half-finished conversation bites the dust. I'm afraid duty calls. Young Jason Lowe has come off his bike—cuts and abrasions. Sounds like a longish clean-up operation so let's get cracking.'

Gemma followed him out into the corridor.

Lowe! Shirley Lowe, query prolapsed uterus, had been one of the patients she'd seen on her first morning.

'Is he one of Shirley Lowe's brood?'

'That's right. She'll bawl him out for cycling too fast, then kiss him to death. Good mother, Shirley.'

Thirteen-year-old Jason was big and bouncy like his mum. He managed to keep some sort of smile on his face during most of the time it took for Sam and Gemma to work on his extensive grazes, though at times it was rather a grim smile. He had skidded on his left side, causing abrasions and what amounted to first-degree burns from his cheek to his ankle.

Slowly, painstakingly, working side by side—Gemma on the leg, Sam on the boy's face and arm—they used forceps to pick out minute pieces of gravel and dirt from the sore areas, and then gently swabbed them clean with an antiseptic. As always, they worked together in perfect, professional harmony.

Sam had to stitch a small, deep cut on Jason's cheek-bone, just below his eye. 'You were lucky there, old son,' he said, as he put in the last stitch. 'Just missed injuring your eye. I'm going to take a look a look in it to make sure that it hasn't been damaged.'

Taking his time, he examined Jason's eye carefully through the ophthalmoscope and pronounced it clear.

He slanted a glance at Gemma. 'All finished at my end. How are you doing, Nurse?'

His words were formal, but his voice was husky, warm…intimate, Gemma thought, her heart hammering out an extra beat.

She straightened up. 'Just finished, Doctor,' she said, matching his formality, 'but I'm not happy about leaving the leg uncovered. Jason's wearing shorts now, but he'll be wearing trousers to school and they're going to rub those sore places.'

Sam nodded. 'Yes, I agree.'

'The best thing,' he explained to Jason, 'would be to leave the wounds exposed—they tend to heal better that way. But, as Nurse pointed out, you'll be wearing trousers to school so we'll have to cover the sore areas with some specially treated dressings to keep them clean and promote healing.'

'If I didn't go to school,' said Jason, grinning cheekily at Sam and Gemma, and at his mother who had just arrived, 'I wouldn't have to wear trousers, would I?'

Shirley lightly cuffed the good side of his face. 'That's enough cheek,' she said severely, though her face was wreathed in a smile of relief. 'It's school for you tomorrow, if Dr Sam thinks that's OK.'

'That's fine by me,' said Sam, 'but don't go kicking a ball around for a day or two, Jason, and make an appointment to come back to see Nurse in five days' time to have your stitches out and the dressings checked.' He stripped off his plastic gloves and tossed them into the bin. 'Now I'm off to see some of my other patients. Nurse will fix you up with dressings.' And with a nod to Shirley and Gemma, he was gone.

Gemma spent the rest of the morning making up for lost time and didn't even snatch a coffee-break. Remembering her promise to Ellie to fill her in on Neil's visit yesterday, she was relieved for the reprieve. Not that it would last. Ellie would expect the full story over their usual lunchtime coffee.

As it happened, she had a further reprieve. When she went into the waiting room to summon her last patient, Mrs Mallory was manning the desk.

'Poor Ellie has a raging toothache and has gone to the dentist,' she explained. 'I've told her to take the afternoon off, so I'm holding the fort for the rest of the day.'

The phone was ringing as Gemma let herself into the cottage at lunchtime. She stared at it till the answerphone clicked on. Before he spoke, she knew that it was Sam. His clear tenor voice filled the small hall.

'Gemma, this is Sam. I won't see you this afternoon. Doing a stint at Shillingbourne Cottage in Theatre. But we must talk. Will call about ninish after Daisy's tucked up. If I don't hear from you, will assume this is OK.'

In between patients, as she worked her way through her list that afternoon, she debated with herself whether to leave a message saying no, or not to ring, which was the same as saying yes. By the time she collected Daisy from school she'd decided not to ring… Sam was right, they *had* to talk.

CHAPTER EIGHT

GEMMA had a tray loaded with bubbling coffee and a plateful of savoury and chocolate biscuits at the ready when Sam arrived at ten. One look at him and the words 'You're an hour overdue—this is a funny sort of nine o'clock' died on her lips.

She led him through to the sitting room, and said firmly, 'You'd better sit down before you fall down. You look exhausted.'

She had been psyching herself up for this meeting all afternoon, but from the moment she had opened the door and seen him, her nervousness had vanished. He'd looked tired this morning, but now... She recognised the drained look. 'Did something happen in Theatre?' she asked, her voice soft, gentle.

Sam sank down into the squashy armchair. 'Last patient on the list, young woman, girl really, only seventeen, appendicectomy, should have been quite straightforward. Well, it was, until she arrested—twice—just as we were finishing off.'

Gemma poured fragrant black coffee, handed him a cup and offered the biscuits. 'Take a handful—you need a sugar boost. Did she...?' Her eyes asked what her lips could not.

Sam shook his head. 'No. We resusced her both times, but it was touch and go, still is. She's in pretty poor shape in Intensive Care. The billion dollar question is—why? Why the sudden collapse? Why did her heart suddenly succumb to the strain of a simple operation? Heart, lungs—everything—appeared normal when Roger Hayes, the anaesthetist, examined her on admission... It only left one real possibility...'

'Cerebral embolism or aneurism?' Gemma whispered.

'Yep. We took some X-rays and it turned out to be an embolism. It showed up clearly, but no way could poor old Roger have known about it. The girl hadn't a history of headaches or dizziness or anything associated with a blocked artery to the brain. Having surgery apparently just triggered it off, and the strain of the extra pressure was too much for her heart even though it had previously been ticking over fine.'

He stared down at his coffee, his hair gleaming in the lamplight. A hank of it fell over his high forehead and Gemma longed to stroke it back.

He lifted his head and stared at her, his eyes full of sadness. 'So frightening to see this fit, sporty girl lying there in the ICU, just hanging on. Poor kid. I saw her this afternoon when I was doing a round on the ward, and she told me how much she was looking forward to running a marathon in aid of leukaemia sufferers in six weeks' time. Wanted to know if she would be fit enough to run by then. Fat chance of that now even if...'

'She survives?'

'Yes.' He looked grim. 'For God's sake, she's had a stroke, Gemma, a girl of seventeen. From the position of the block, it looks as if she'll have left-side paralysis. She's an athlete. What is she going to do with her life when she's half-paralysed?'

'Sam, I know it's a cliché, where there's life and so on—but it's true.' She laid a hand on his arm—a comforting hand, a small enough gesture when she would have liked to have held him close, kissed his stiff, cold lips and warmed them. 'We've both seen things like that happen before, for no rhyme nor reason, and patients come through. And there's so much being done for stroke victims now, especially young ones. There's no reason why she shouldn't make a complete recovery. It is possible.'

He stared down at her hand resting on his arm, and then up into her face. His eyes brightened a little. 'You're dead right, of course. Not only might she pull through, but she might make a full recovery. I needed to hear that. I can think of some women who would have bawled me out for being late, but you didn't. You've even let me talk about it.' His lips curved into the semblance of a smile. 'I'm grateful.'

Gemma smiled back. 'No need to be. I'm a nurse.'

Some women would have bawled him out! Women he knew intimately? Stop second-guessing! There was no reason to suppose there were a host of other women in his life now, even if, according to Gloria Watson, there'd been plenty in the past, and one of them had been special. No, Gloria hadn't said that, she'd said… Oh, what did it matter what she'd said? It was only gossip.

There's no smoke without fire, whispered a nasty little voice at the back of her head.

Of course he was attractive to, and attracted by, women, and treated them with a special courtesy. But, then, so did his father—it was part of the Mallory charm. Not that it was anything like Neil's hollow charm—was it?

As for his social life outside the surgery, that was a mystery. Perhaps in his rare off-duty periods he pursued a wild life in Shorehampton or Bournemouth, but if he did she knew nothing of it. In fact, she knew very little about any part of his life when he wasn't working, except what he'd told her on that glorious kite-flying Saturday afternoon, and that had all been about family—his parents and his brother and two sisters...

'Do you think I might have another coffee, please?' Sam was holding out his empty cup and wearing a quizzical, lopsided smile. He was looking a little less tense.

Gemma snapped out of her reverie. Her cheeks reddened. 'Oh, yes, of course,' she said breathily, taking his cup and crossing to the side table to fill it.

Had he noticed that for a moment she'd been lost in thought? Her hand shook slightly as she poured. What had she been thinking about, letting her mind wander when Sam was eaten up with concern for his patient? *Some nurse—some confidante!* How could she?

She handed him his brimming cup. Behave as if nothing happened, get back to basics. 'Any chance of finding out what caused the embolism, or is it going to remain a mystery?'

Sam took a huge swallow of coffee. 'Might do. They'll run a huge battery of tests and might come up with some answers. But as you reminded me, in our line of work the unforseen, the unexpected can happen, and sometimes there isn't an obvious answer. It's the sort of nightmare situation we have to live with, leaving one always wondering if one could have done just that little bit more. Poor Roger's worried witless, wondering if he missed something when he examined her.'

'Could he have?'

Sam shook his head. 'Not very likely, he's very experienced, thorough, an excellent anaesthetist. But it's always possible, though there was nothing in the girl's history to indicate that anything might go wrong. She was admitted yesterday, had the usual four-hourly obs taken—all were normal. No abnormalities in the blood tests that were taken. She's an athlete in the peak of fitness. The embolism was a freak accident. All that we can do now is hope she pulls through.'

He looked at his watch and frowned. 'Wonder how she's doing?' He looked across at Gemma as though she might have the answer.

'Why don't you ring and find out?' she suggested practically.

The frown disappeared, to be replaced by a brief smile. 'Brilliant idea,' he said, as if she'd suggested phoning the moon. 'Why didn't I think of that?'

Because you're pretty shattered, she thought, and clever men like you often miss the obvious.

He pulled his mobile out of his pocket and punched in a number.

Gemma busied herself gathering up the dirty cups and empty biscuit plate—he'd eaten the lot. She heard him ask if Dr Hayes was still there—apparently he was. Sam asked to speak to him.

'Would you like a sandwich?' she mouthed, while he was waiting to be connected.

'Please.' He touched the back of her hand with his fingertips. It was a fleeting, featherlight touch, but her skin was still tingling when she reached the kitchen.

She made a pile of chicken sandwiches, armed herself with two glasses and the half bottle of whisky she had denied Neil, and returned to the sitting room.

Sam was perched on the edge of his chair, his mobile still in his hand. His face was unreadable. Good news or bad? Let it be good! He's had enough for one day.

'Well?' Her voice came out a breathy whisper.

He stood up and pocketed his mobile and stared at her as if surprised to see her. 'She's holding her own, seems to have stabilised. Not out of the woods yet, but if she maintains the status quo for another hour they reckon she'll be fit enough to be helicoptered down to Bournemouth for specialised assessment and treatment.' His mouth tilted in a tentative smile. 'It's better than we could have hoped for a few hours ago.'

'Oh, Sam, I'm so glad. The sooner she can have treatment the better. It'll give her a fighting chance of overcoming the paralysis, won't it?'

'That's the latest thinking—to get cracking on massage, physiotherapy and speech therapy within hours of a cerebral accident taking place. And as you reminded me just now, some patients make a remarkable recovery. Please, God, it's true of this youngster.'

His blue gaze, soft and melting, melded with hers. 'Oh, Gemma.' He reached out and took both her hands in his. He raised them to his lips and brushed a kiss across her knuckles. Then he drew her into his arms and cradled her head against his chest.

It felt familiar, she felt at home. His heart beat firmly but a little fast beneath her ear. He nuzzled the top of her head with his nose and his lips and his chin. It felt incredibly sweet, safe, being there in his arms. They stood together for seemingly endless minutes, swaying gently, clinging together, supporting each other.

This is how it should be, she thought, each of us supporting the other. How can you possibly know that? You hardly know each other, and supposing there was something in what the Watson woman said? protested a small, sober little voice. Supposing there was something in his past and he wasn't the perfect man, the perfect doctor. Her heart told her that it didn't matter.

'Doesn't this feel *right*?' murmured Sam, echoing her thoughts, his breath stirring her hair.

'Mmm...just what I was thinking.' She burrowed deeper against his chest and the long, strong column of his throat.

'We're on the same wavelength, Gemma, have been since that first morning when we met.' His voice was muffled, buried in her hair. He lifted his head and put a finger beneath her chin and tilted it upwards. 'A few weeks ago...a lifetime ago...but time doesn't matter, we belong together, my love.'

The pretty little carriage clock inherited from her great-aunt Marjorie gave out eleven silvery chimes—and then there was silence, a velvet-deep silence.

For a moment, as if they were one, almost drowning in each other's eyes, they both held their breath.

A dozen thoughts raced and tumbled around in Gemma's head just as her heart seemed to tumble round in her chest, refusing to be still. She struggled to get her thoughts together. What did he mean, belong together? Was he talking marriage or something else? And what about Daisy, her baby—where did she fit in? Had he forgotten Daisy? The small voice fired out one question after another.

It was all very romantic, talking about time not mattering. Perhaps it didn't to the two of them, but it did to Daisy. With Neil as a role model for a father, she would need *time*, and plenty of it, to accept a man into her life...or anyone perhaps on a permanent basis.

Her world revolves around you! reminded her voice loud and clear.

If he's suggesting marriage or a partnership. Her thoughts faltered as she was drawn deeper and deeper into the blue pools of his eyes. Perhaps he didn't mean that, perhaps he means just sex...

She swam up to the surface and exhaled her long held breath, breaking the silence. 'What do you mean?' she whispered. 'Belong together? I don't understand.'

Amusement flared in Sam's eyes. 'My word,' he murmured, 'the wheels have been churning. I could almost read your thoughts...'

Could he? Her cheeks went pink...

'There's no mystery, my love. Belonging together means what it says—I belong to you,

you belong to me. You and me and Daisy, together.'

'Oh,' The word was breathy and drawn out. 'You didn't forget Daisy!'

'Bloody hell, do you think I would?' His voice was suddenly cold. He eased away from her and put his hands on her shoulders. '*Did you, Gemma?*'

A shutter slammed down over his eyes, leaving them cold to match his cold voice. Gemma shivered and felt the blood drain from her cheeks. He was so angry.

'I—I—' she stuttered. 'I didn't know… You see, Neil—'

'What's Neil got to do with it? You're supposed to be divorced, but he's always hanging around.' Sam's voice was icy. 'Have you still got a *thing* for him, Gemma? Tell me honestly.'

His eyes bored into hers, his fingers bit into her shoulders.

The biting fingers rallied her. She said quietly, 'You're hurting me, Sam.'

He swore beneath his breath and released his hold on her shoulders. 'Oh, Gemma, my dear love, I'm so sorry—the last thing I want to do is to hurt you, but that man makes my hackles rise.'

'But you don't know him.'

'Don't need to,' he ground out. 'A maniac who drives like he does and has obviously damaged you in the past—that's enough for me. Dear God, the thought of him and you...'

Her heart gave a leap. She wanted to wipe the pain off his face, the pain that said as clearly as if he had spoken...I love you, it proclaimed loud and clear.

She said very gently, 'Sam, there is no him and me. He has access rights to see Daisy, that's all, and he only exercises them when the mood takes him. He isn't a very good father, never was, couldn't face up to his responsibilities, opted out soon after Daisy was born. Comes back to play daddy occasionally, but sometimes it's months between visits.'

He cupped her face in his hands. 'Is that why you found it hard to believe that I included Daisy in my future plans for us, because he has no sense of responsibility?'

'Yes. Oh, Sam, I'm so afraid for Daisy, she's had so many ups and downs in her short life. He's made promises that he hasn't kept, sometimes spoils her, sometimes ignores her, sometimes even frightens her...'

Incredulity, horror, anger flared in his eyes. 'Do you mean he threatens her physically?'

'Do you think I'd let him? No, in spite of his temper he's never done that. Rather the reverse. He's sometimes too affectionate and retreats into a stony silence if Daisy doesn't respond as he thinks she should. And that frightens her and makes her feel guilty for upsetting him. He's like a chameleon. She doesn't know what it's like to have a man around who is solid, dependable.'

Sam kissed her nose. 'I'd be solid and dependable, Gemma. Just give me a chance to prove it.' His voice was husky, his lovely blue eyes, warm and tender, devoured her. With his thumbs he traced the contours of her cheekbones. He kissed her eyelids. 'You're a beautiful woman, my darling, and you've been on your own too long. All I want to do is to take care of you and Daisy, and the sooner I can start the better.'

My darling! And said so tenderly, it sounded good. Too good to be true?

'Fine words butter no parsnips.' Gemma recalled the words of a dear old lady whom she had nursed. 'What does it mean?' she had asked. 'It's easy to make promises, quite another matter to put them into practice,' old Mrs Thompson had explained tartly.

A little shiver of apprehension ran up and down Gemma's spine. Was Sam making rash promises that he wouldn't be able to put into practice? He was a fancy-free bachelor. Did he really want to give up that freedom to care for her and Daisy? And *if* he had let one woman down... She should ask him if it was true. She would, but not now. He'd had enough for one evening. And so had she. She couldn't bear it if...

All that mattered was Daisy's happiness. Everything was happening too fast. The bottom line was—

'Gemma, come back to me, please.' Sam's voice, soft but firm, lasered through her thoughts. He dropped his hands from her face and moved back a step as if sensing that she needed space. 'Tell me what's wrong.'

He sounded so kind, so understanding—everything Neil was not. 'How do you know that anything's wrong?' she countered, trying a tentative smile.

'Your beautiful eyes and face are a dead give-away, they're very expressive, so, please, tell me what I can do to make things right.'

'Give us time, much more time. It's all so unreal. We know so little about each other. Daisy especially needs time. I won't be rushed, I must be sure that she likes you and trusts you enough to—' The words came tumbling out in a rush.

'Let me in?'

'Yes. There's just been the two of us for so long. I'd be a rotten mother if I rushed things just because…' She flushed a little. 'Because you and I, on the strength of hormones and vibes—'

'Have fallen in love and want to be together?'

Gemma moistened her lips with the tip of her tongue. 'Yes,' she whispered.

Sam's mouth crooked into a lopsided smile. 'Then we won't rush things. We will be old-fashioned and conventional and take time to get to know each other. I will court you, and after a decent interval propose, with Daisy's love and approval. For I intend to win her love, Gemma, and I intend being the best father in the world to her, make no mistake about that.

She will be loved and cherished as every child should be.'

He cupped her chin in his hands again and looked down into her upturned face. 'You do believe me, Gemma, don't you? *I* keep the promises I make.'

His sweetness made her want to cry. But should she...? No, she had no doubts. 'Yes, Sam, I believe you. Thank you for understanding.'

'What's to understand? It's what mature love is all about, keeping promises. I'm no youngster mistaking lust for love, or a man who has never grown up to appreciate what commitment is. I won't let you or Daisy down, dear heart.' He kissed her gently on the mouth as the carriage clock chimed the half-hour. 'And now I'm away while we're still on the respectable side of midnight, or tongues will start wagging too hard. They'll start soon enough anyway—someone's bound to have seen me arrive.'

Gemma laughed a little uncertainly. 'Why will they wag?'

Sam gave a deep-throated chuckle. 'Because we're news. We're not in the big city now. We'll be the talk of the village, the young doctor, whom many of them have known since he was a baby, and the beautiful new nurse. Lovely, juicy gossiping point, even in this day and age.'

Gemma said drily, 'I suppose they'll rate me as a sort of seductress, you know, the gay divorcee out to get her man. As long as Daisy—'

'Daisy won't suffer, love. You've already established yourself as a good mother and a kind and caring nurse. The gossip will be curious but kind so, please, don't worry about it. Now, I'm really off. Goodnight, my love, sleep well. Thanks for the coffee and sympathy and, most of all, thank you for loving me.'

He gave her another quick kiss, whisked himself out of the room and moments later she heard the front door close behind him.

She went to bed prepared, almost hoping, to lie awake for hours, mulling over the evening's events. She wanted to examine it minutely, from the moment Sam had arrived to when he had said goodnight. But she got no further than when Sam had wrapped her in his arms and held her against his broad chest. Remembering his heart beating a little fast but strongly beneath her ear, she was lulled to sleep, and slept

till Daisy bounced into her room at seven
o'clock next morning.

Daisy was full of chat about the day ahead.
'Don't forget that Katy's coming to tea,
Mummy.'

Gemma smiled down into the bright, beaming face. 'I haven't forgotten, love. What do
you think she would like to eat?'

'Fish fingers and baked beans—they're her
favourites.'

'Right, so shall it be. And what about pudding?'

'Strawberry ice cream with a banana cut into
circles. Oh, and gingerbread men.'

Thank God for simple tastes, thought
Gemma, giving Daisy a hug and a kiss. 'I think
we can manage that, kiddo.'

Having deposited Daisy safely at school,
Gemma made her way, her head bent deep in
thought, towards the surgery.

After last night how were she and Sam to
greet each other, work together? Would it be
embarrassing? And his parents—how would
they react to the situation? They'd made her
so welcome as a member of the staff, but how

would they feel about her as a potential daughter-in-law?

She tried to picture it from their angle. A single mum with a small daughter, whom they hardly knew. Surely they would feel that their beloved eldest son was making a mistake. And what about Ellie, who had confided in her and had a crush on Sam—would she feel that Gemma had betrayed her?

Sam had made it all sound so easy. He would court her—nice old-fashioned word, 'court'. Daisy would get to know him, learn to love him, everything would be wonderful. All part of the miracle that had brought her to Blaney St Mary.

'Hi, isn't it a perfectly *beautiful* morning?'

Gemma jerked up her head. Sam's voice was husky, a tone lower than usual, rich with double meaning. He was walking towards her, with Rufus and Rex, the family Labradors, loping along on either side of him. He stopped just in front of her. The dogs sniffed at her with their soft muzzles and waved feathery tails.

Gemma stroked their silky heads, and her heart, already churning as her turbulent thoughts whizzed round in her head, churned some more as her eyes feasted on the man before her. He stood tall, lean, muscular, his bright fair hair glowing in the early morning sunlight and enhanced by a turtle-necked creamy sweater.

Memory stirred as Gemma stared. Substitute silver armour for the creamy sweater and he was a double for the picture of Sir Galahad, the gallant knight in her favourite book of legends which she'd drooled over as a child.

She made her lips move. 'Yes,' she breathed. 'It *is* a beautiful morning, but—'

'But?'

'Why are you out walking the dogs at this hour?' Her voice remained a breathy whisper.

'It's my late start morning—first patient's booked for nine-thirty.'

Gemma cleared her throat. 'I know, but you usually catch up on paperwork and phone calls on late start mornings.'

Sam's eyes, incredibly blue, incredibly warm, twinkled like mad. 'This morning I decided to break with tradition and go to meet my love, and be seen to be courting.' He leaned forward and tucked a strand of hair, lifted by the light breeze, carefully behind her ear. A casual gesture, but he made it seem like a caress.

'Oh.' The breathiness was back. Gemma glanced quickly round to see if they were being observed. There were a few people walking their dogs and a few children dawdling to school.

Sam chuckled. 'Nervous of attracting attention, love? Well, I dare say there are a few lace curtains twitching, and that innocent gesture will start tongues wagging. But does it matter? The sooner everyone gets used to seeing us around together, the better.' His eyes swept over her face. 'You don't mind, do you, Gemma?' He touched her cheek lightly with his fingertips. 'As I said last night, any gossip will be friendly gossip.'

Gemma touched the spot on her cheek that he had touched. Her eyes smiled into his. 'No, Sam,' she said softly, lingering over his name. 'I don't mind, just as long as Daisy isn't harmed by rumours before I can explain to her about you and me.' She forced her eyes away from his and fumbled for her fob watch beneath her jacket.

'Lord, I shall be late. We'll have to talk some other time.' She began walking quickly towards the surgery.

Sam and the two dogs fell in beside her. 'This evening?' he asked. His face curved into a smile. 'And I promise you, rather earlier and less harrowing than last night—before Daisy goes to bed. Just a casual visit, like the other night when I dropped in. That was quite a success. Perhaps we could fix something for the weekend, as we did then, not kite-flying this time but something else. There's a steam rally over at Lower Boxley, with a train for the kids to ride on. Daisy would love that. How about it, Gemma?'

They reached the surgery and walked round the side of the building to the staff door. His hand brushed against hers and she shivered with the sheer pleasure of his flesh touching hers.

'Cold?' he asked, his eyes flaring with amusement.

Gemma shook her head. He knows that I'm not, she thought.

He dropped the dogs' leads. 'Stay,' he commanded. They lay down, their heads resting on their paws. 'Good boys.'

He turned to Gemma and held wide his arms. 'Come here,' he said softly, but still with a note of command in his voice.

'We shouldn't, not here...' Gemma murmured and stepped forward into his arms.

For a few moments he held her as he had the previous night, cradling her head against his heart. He kissed the top of her head then tilted her face and kissed her mouth, his tongue teasing her lips apart to explore the soft, moist interior. Their tongues entwined, their warm breath mingled.

Gemma's legs felt as if they might give way. She could hardly breathe. With an effort she pulled her face away from his. 'Must go,' she muttered. 'Please, Sam, let me go.'

He rubbed his nose to hers and let his arms fall to his sides. 'I love you,' he said, and, picking up the dogs' leads, turned and walked away.

CHAPTER NINE

GEMMA tidied herself up in the cloakroom, running a comb through her hair and touching up her 'kiss-proof'—not against *that* sort of kiss—lipstick over her smudged, bruised lips. She stared into the mirror over the basin, trying to assess if anyone would notice that she had been so thoroughly kissed. The dreamy look in her smoky green eyes was a dead give-away, she thought, smiling at her reflection. But what the dickens? She was feeling on top of the world.

She went through to Reception to collect her list, and came down from cloud nine with a jolt. Olivia Mallory was manning the desk. Normally, working with Mrs M. was a joy, but this morning was nowhere near normal, and the last person she wanted to see was Sam's mother, and be inspected by those kind but shrewd hazel eyes. What on earth would she have thought had she seen her practice nurse wrapped in her son's arms, being kissed senseless, only minutes before?

Gemma's heart beat a tattoo against her ribs, and her puffy lips felt dry as she approached the desk and arranged a smile on her face. 'Hello, Mrs M. This is a surprise. I thought Ellie would be back this morning.' Her voice, meant to sound bright and breezy and, oh, so casual, came out sounding as if she had a bad dose of tonsillitis. She cleared her throat.

Olivia Mallory glanced up from the pile of records she was dealing with and gave her a quick wide smile, just like Sam's, then pulled a face. 'Poor Ellie. She expected to be back, but she had a rough time when she saw her dentist yesterday. He found an abscess beneath the tooth that was giving her pain. She's on penicillin but is feeling pretty ropey so I've told her to take a couple of days off.'

'Poor old Ellie. And poor you. Weren't you going to meet a friend in Bournemouth tomorrow to go shopping?'

'With luck, I still will. Helen Brodie's back from holiday and has agreed to hold the fort tomorrow. You haven't met her yet—she's our occasional relief receptionist.'

Gemma nodded. 'Yes, I know. Ellie's mentioned the name. I look forward to meeting her.' She glanced at her watch. 'Goodness, I'd better get cracking or my patients will think I've deserted them.' She picked up her list and fled to the treatment room away from those shrewd eyes.

By concentrating like mad, she managed to keep her tumultuous thoughts at bay as she worked her way through her list of patients.

It was a mixed bag, starting with a couple of cervical smears, women who hadn't been able to get to the regular session the previous week. Both were perfectly straightforward and easily dealt with.

They were followed by Jamie Hooper, a small boy with stitches to be removed from his knee. It was a tearful episode, but mercifully brief, with Jamie brightening up as soon as it was over and Gemma offered him the sweetie jar. He chose a green lolly, and cheekily admitted to his mother, who had been even more nervous than he, that it hadn't hurt much. She hugged him and told him that he was a brave boy, and with effusive thanks to Gemma led him away with promises of more goodies to come.

Tidying up in readiness for the next patient, Gemma thought how apt the saying was that children made cowards of us all. For a split second she thought of Daisy. When would she have the courage to break the news to her daughter that they would be seeing a lot more of Sam in the future and that he might become a more permanent fixture in their lives? How would Daisy take it? Would she hate the idea? And if she did, what then?

Sam! Just thinking about him, it made her pulses race and her cheeks flush. Furiously squashing the thought and willing the blush to subside, she went out to the waiting room to call in her next patient.

Elderly Mrs Green was anaemic and had come in for her monthly injection of iron. She'd had several previous injections, but remained nervous about them.

'That nurse who was here for a short while a few months ago hurt me something awful,' she said. 'Gave me a dreadful bruise. Mind you, to be fair, I do bruise easy.'

'Then I'll be extra careful,' Gemma promised as she swabbed the upper and outer quadrant of the elderly buttock with antiseptic. Then, holding the muscle firm, she popped in the wide-bore needle and slowly released the Imferon that she had drawn up into the syringe.

A few minutes later, exclaiming that she'd hardly felt a thing, a relieved Mrs Green left the treatment room.

The rest of the morning was busy, and Gemma didn't even stop for coffee. It was nearly one o'clock and she was clearing up after her last patient when Sam appeared in the doorway.

Her heart gyrated as his eyes feasted hungrily upon her.

'I was hoping,' he murmured, his rich tenor voice warm and husky, 'that we might have lunched together, but I have an emergency call-out and I'll have to go straight on to take surgery at Little Wickford after I've sorted it out, so I won't see you till tonight, my love.'

My love! He made it sound so proprietorial, as if only he had the right to say it. She wanted to leap across the room and throw herself into his arms, feel them wrapped hard around her as they had been this morning. She wouldn't see him till tonight... Tonight seemed a lifetime away.

'Oh, well, not to worry,' she heard herself say in an airy, doesn't-matter sort of voice. 'I've oodles to do in my lunch hour.'

Sam's vivid blue eyes twinkled with laughter. She might have known he'd see right through her. Bravado, that's all it was and he knew it. She felt her own eyes twinkling back at him—it was wonderful being on the same wavelength, the right vibes winging their way between them... Please, let Daisy—

Sam said softly, 'I've got to go, dear heart, but I promise you all is going to be well.' Lifting his hand in a farewell salute, he turned and walked away down the corridor.

Dear heart! My love! He made them sound so precious, made her feel so special. It was like being in love for the first time. Her cheeks flamed, her heart stood still—she *was* in love for the first time.

What about Neil—hadn't he been her first love? *No!* It was crystal clear. What she had felt for Neil hadn't been love. Not true love. He had needed mothering, or something like that. It was hard to remember. Sex had come into it, but not this overwhelming, consuming passion that she felt for Sam.

Yet this was a passion that was about more than sex—a passion to share everything, to be as one. To care for each other and care for Daisy.

She did a little pirouette of sheer joy, finished clearing up, called goodbye to Mrs M., who was on the phone, and let herself out through the staff door.

It was true that she had oodles do in her lunch hour. She'd promised Daisy that she would make gingerbread men for their tea that night. She prepared the ginger biscuit mix whilst eating a sandwich and gulping down a cup of coffee. In the middle of rolling out the mixture it suddenly dawned on her that, with Katy coming to tea, Sam wouldn't be able to visit.

Her heart plummeted.

'Oh, no,' she groaned. 'Why didn't I think about about it before?'

She knew why. Because she longed to have Sam there in her own house, wanted to see him sitting at her table playing silly games with Daisy, as he had before, looking as if he belonged. And because he had bewitched her when he had uttered the words 'my love' and 'dear heart' with that particular throb in his voice, leaving her breathless and tongue-tied.

Well, she would have to untie her tongue and ring him and tell him not to come. She groaned again. It was the last thing she wanted to do so she'd better get on with it while she had the strength of mind to do so.

She picked up the receiver and rang his mobile. He answered on the second buzz.

She blurted out quickly, 'Sam, I won't keep you a moment, but don't come tonight. Daisy's got a schoolfriend coming for tea.'

'So...why should that stop me?' He sounded amused, his voice drawling.

'Well... Because...' she faltered. 'I don't know really, it's just that...' Her voice petered out.

'One small girl will go home and tell her mummy that Dr Sam visited Daisy's house. Is that what it is, Gemma?'

He was laughing at her, teasing her. She hadn't expected that. What had happened to the vibes, the being as one? A wave of anger and bewilderment washed over her. She could picture his face, his twinkling eyes, his wide curving smile. Why was he laughing at her? Didn't he realise that she was worried because of Daisy? Daisy would be—

'Are you all right, love?' his voice was no longer teasing, but soft and gentle.

She wanted to shout, No, I'm *not* all right. I'm mixed up and anxious and feel guilty because I let myself fall in love with you. And for all I know you might be as bad as Neil and go off and leave us, like he did, like you left that girl. But the words wouldn't come, they stuck in her throat.

'Gemma?' He sounded puzzled. 'Look, if it bothers you that much, I won't come tonight but, please, tell me what's wrong. Is it Daisy?'

His tender tone melted her insides, turned them to mush.

'Yes, it's Daisy... I'm so afraid that she will be hurt by the gossip.' Her voice was a wobbly whisper. 'I know you said she wouldn't be, but...' Her voice almost dried up, then she blurted out, 'Is it true—did you desert a girl when you were younger?'

She almost dropped the receiver. She was appalled. She shouldn't have asked him over the phone—perhaps she shouldn't have asked him at all. Yes, she should. For Daisy's sake— her own sake—she had to know. She stared at the the silent phone. 'Sam...'Her voice shook. 'I must know.'

'Of course you must.' His voice was flat. 'But it was so long ago...'

'You thought that I'd never hear about it?' Her mouth felt dry, sour.

'No, Gemma, because it was an unpleasant incident that happened a long time ago and isn't relevant to us. I certainly wasn't deliberately hiding anything. I would have told you about it some time when we were exchanging mutual histories.' He spoke coolly, rationally.

'Some time!' The bitter taste in her mouth came through in her voice. This was the man who had seemed to be flawless. 'Would you, I wonder?' She made an effort to pull herself together. 'But I musn't keep you, you're working.'

'I'm in the surgery and haven't opened up yet, though I can hear patients arriving.' He paused for a moment. 'Gemma, I must come tonight. I don't know what gossip you've heard, but you should hear the full unabridged version before condemning me out of hand. I'll come after Daisy's friend has gone, if you prefer.'

She made up her mind suddenly. Never let it be said that she hadn't given him a fair hearing. 'No—come as you planned, sixish.' She gave a funny, cracked little laugh. 'I'll save you a gingerbread man.'

'I *love* gingerbread men.'

* * *

The afternoon seemed endless. There was an empty, cold space in Gemma's chest where her heart should have been, but the world went on. Patients still needed attention.

She had just finished treating her last patient on the afternoon list when Dr Mallory rang through and asked her to clean and dress a foot wound.

'And give him a shot of anti-tetanus, and codeine for the pain. But don't be late collecting Daisy from school,' he said in his usual courteous, thoughtful manner. 'Old Harry will be happy to wait for me to see to him after I've finished here if you can't manage it.'

Gemma assured him that it was no problem. She had plenty of time—one of her patients hadn't shown up. 'So who is old Harry?' she asked.

'Trotter.'

'Should I know him?'

Dr Mallory chuckled. 'Probably not. He's on our list, but not what you would call a regular. Last saw him officially about five years ago when his wife died, though I drop in on him from time to time. He lives about three miles from the village. He's ninety-five and hiked in this afternoon to have his foot looked at.'

'*Hiked!* With an injured foot?'

'That's Harry, a tough old bird. Wouldn't have come but thought he was bleeding a bit too much, and it was giving him gyp—his word to express what must be excruciating pain. Just as well it bled—washed some of the muck out of it. I've dowsed it with antiseptic and put on a temporary pad and the bleeding's eased, but it needs a Kaltostat dressing and a protective pad.'

'How did he injure his foot?'

'Sliced into it with the edge of a sharp spade just below and between his big toe and the next toe, in the soft tissue between the meta-tarsus. Went right through his wellie, might well have had a couple of toes off. He nicked a blood vessel but miraculously seems to have missed the tendons and bones, though I don't know how.'

'Oh, well, an X-ray will show if they're damaged...'

'An X-ray.' There was a chuckle at the other end of the phone. 'I suggested it, of course, but Harry flatly refused. Short of manhandling him to the hospital, there's nothing I can do about it. But the old boy's probably right about there being no long-term damage. He knows the score. He's had many minor, and not so minor, injuries over the years and has survived them virtually unaided. But I've put him on an antibiotic and threatened him on pain of death to complete the course.'

He paused, then added, 'Take good care of him, Gemma. He's rather a special old guy, he's known me since I was a baby—that's sixty-odd years ago. He was already a married man with a family when I was born. Knew me as the young Dr James, just as Sam is now known as the young doctor.'

There was another pause, then he said softly, 'He was at our wedding, you know, together with most of the village. And who knows? If Sam gets his act together and doesn't leave it too long, he'll be at *his* wedding, too. And that would please the old boy nearly as much as it would please us.' He cleared his throat and became suddenly brisk. 'But that's enough of this maudlin nonsense. I'll leave Harry in your capable hands, my dear.'

Or not so capable, Gemma thought, replacing the receiver with hands that trembled slightly. She was shaken by Dr Mallory's potted family history, especially his reference to Sam and marriage. Marriage to Sam. This morning when he had kissed her it had been practically a dead cert. Now, because of listening to Gloria's gossip, she was hovering on the brink of—

The thought pulled her up short. What was she thinking about? Whatever Sam's explanation for something that had happened in the distant past, and whether or not she accepted it; their relationship had hardly got off the ground, and as yet Daisy knew nothing about it. Daisy was the important factor. Other people hardly mattered, not even the kind, benevolent Mallorys, whose approval she would like to have. It was for Daisy's sake she had to know the truth.

She took a deep breath. Enough thinking— better get cracking and get on with work. Nice, straightforward work—she knew where she was with that.

Thank God for antibiotics and anti-tetanus, she thought a few minutes later as she bent over Mr Trotter's foot. She removed the pressure pad that Dr Mallory had left *in situ*, revealing a mucky wound which looked as if it could do with all the protective cover on offer.

The bleeding had stopped, leaving a gungy mess of dirt and dried blood in the long cut carved by the corner of the sharp spade. She sprayed analgesic round the wound, then, using a needleless syringe to squirt in normal saline, she swabbed away the dirty effluent as it oozed out.

Old Harry watched with interest, seemingly indifferent to the pain that the procedure must be causing in spite of the analgesic spray.

Gemma sniffed. She recognised that smell from her schooldays. Riding lessons—stables—horses—manure! She wrinkled her nose and glanced up at the old man.

'Would I be right in thinking you were digging in horse manure when you sliced into your foot, Mr Trotter?'

'That's right, m'dear, I was dunging me roses, nothing like dung for roses.'

Or for bugs, thought Gemma.

'All done,' she announced ten minutes later as she strapped the thick protective pad in position over the Kaltostat dressing. 'But you must come back in five days' time so that I can renew the dressing. Meanwhile, don't get it wet and please don't remove it. This wound's going to take some time to heal.' Carefully she eased his boot on over the bulky dressing.

'It's only a bit of an 'ole,' Mr Trotter replied grumpily. 'It'll mend in no time.'

'It won't if you interfere with it, I can assure you.' Gemma made her voice very firm, but injected into it a note of humour. 'And you'll get me the sack if anything goes wrong with it. Dr Mallory will think that I haven't done my job properly.'

The old man stared at her and ran calloused fingers round his bristly chin. 'You black-mailing me, missus?' he asked, his faded eyes twinkling.

Gemma gave him her nicest smile. 'Could be,' she said cheerfully, 'but the doctor will be mad at me if it doesn't heal, that's for sure.'

'Oh, well, suppose we can't have the old doctor blowing his top—I've a lot of use for the old doctor, and the young 'n too.' He stood up and hobbled toward the door. 'I'll be in next week, m'dear.'

'You do that and make my day,' said

Gemma, with a laugh as he left the room.

He was, as Dr Mallory said, a special old guy.

She tried to still her thoughts as she crossed the green to meet Daisy and Katy from school, but they continued to nag persistently. It had been a day of significant happenings, from Sam's kiss in the morning to the treating of old Harry at the end of the day, which had been triggered off by the conversation with Dr Mallory.

How proud he was of his family's long involvement with the village, underlining the close rapport that he and Sam and Mrs M. had with their patients. And how sure he seemed that it would continue into yet another generation. It implied that their association with Blaney St Mary was set in stone. How did she feel about that? Just supposing, how would Daisy feel if…?

She gave an anguished sigh and a mental shake and shut down on her teeming thoughts as she reached the school gates. The rest of the afternoon would be devoted to the children.

They had just finished tea and were debating which video to watch, *Mary Poppins* or *Snow White*, when the doorbell rang.

Gemma looked at the clock. Just after six—it had to be Sam. She felt queasy. This was going to be quite an ordeal.

She stood up. 'I'll go,' she said, but Daisy beat her to it, slithering down from her chair and racing out into the hall, with Katy hot on her heels. Gemma, her heart thumping painfully in anticipation, brought up the rear. Daisy flung open the door.

Sam, accompanied by Rex and Rufus, was standing in the porch.

The children uttering delighted oohs and ahs, and draped themselves round the necks of the handsome, tail-waving Labradors.

'I was walking the hounds,' Sam explained to Gemma over the girls' heads, 'and I thought that Daisy and her friend might like to meet them.' A smile of sorts touched his lips, but didn't reach his eyes.

Daisy looked up, her face very bright and alert. 'How did you know that Katy would be here, Dr Sam?'

Trust Daisy to see through that little fib. How would Sam explain it away?

Quite simply. 'Because your mummy told me that she had to hurry home at lunchtime to make gingerbread men because your friend was coming to tea.' He grinned down at both girls. 'I love gingerbread men and, to be honest, I came in the hope that there might be one going spare.'

Smooth!

'Oh, there is,' said Daisy enthusiastically. 'There's more than one, isn't there, Mummy?'

Gemma said brightly in the manner of a good hostess, 'There certainly is and Dr Sam is welcome to one, but not out here on the doorstep. Do come in, Sam.'

'And the hounds?'

'Of course, they're most welcome.'

She stood back as he and the dogs, led by Daisy and Katy, filed into the sitting room. His brilliant blue eyes inscrutable, he stared down into her face as he passed. Gemma lowered her head, afraid of what he would read in her eyes. Love, hate, mistrust!

The girls took over the hostessing, stationing Rex and Rufus on the hearthrug and steering Sam to a seat at the table.

Daisy placed a plate of gingerbread men in front of him and pleaded for a game of something. 'Like we had before when you came— cards or junior Trivial Pursuit,' she said.

Gemma said with a high, tinkling laugh, 'Give Dr Sam a moment to catch his breath, love. And perhaps Katy would rather watch a video, as you planned.'

Katy shook her head. 'No, thank you, I'd like to play cards. I can see the video any old time.'

Implying, thought Gemma, that playing cards with the doctor was a treat not to be missed. She felt that the situation was getting away from her, and wondered why she'd insisted that Sam should come as arranged before…before she'd accused him, on the strength of gossip, of deserting some girl in his past. They wouldn't get a chance to talk so what was the point?

'Oh, well, in that case, if the doctor doesn't mind.' She made herself look at Sam and produce a smile. 'Would you like a drink—wine or something stronger?' He didn't look in the least bit rattled, but maybe he was feeling as edgy as she.

He looked down at the tall glasses in front of the girls. He picked a glass up and sniffed it. 'Ginger beer would suit me fine,' he said, to the girls' delight.

Sam knew an endless variety of children's card games. The girls wanted to know how he knew so many games.

'Legacy of my misspent youth, wet afternoons and a large number of younger relatives to be entertained,' he said with a laugh, slickly dealing out cards for Chase the Wicked Lady. He explained the simple rules and they had a noisy, hilarious session.

Occasionally his eyes, still unreadable, met and held Gemma's. Was he angry with her for listening to gossip, and would he be able to explain it away? Please, let him, she prayed inwardly. Don't let him have run away from commitment.

The Wicked Lady was followed by Catch a Thief and Three in a Row. The girls clamoured for more, but an hour later Sam stood up and announced that he must go.

'A doctor's life doesn't end when he sees his last patient for the day,' he said with a laugh, dismissing their entreaties to stay. 'I have phone calls to make, you might call it my homework.'

The girls giggled. 'Homework's for learning things,' said Daisy. 'I thought doctors knew everything.'

'I wish,' Sam replied, pulling a doleful face. 'In my job you go on learning for ever. So I'll be off, ladies. Thanks for the games. You were both brilliant, we'll make card-sharps of you yet.'

'What's a card-sharp?' they asked in unison.

Sam grinned. 'Someone who's sharp at cards,' he said. He called the dogs who were dozing in front of the elegant steel fireplace, filled with a blaze of flowers on this warm spring evening and commanded them to say goodbye. To the girls' delight, Rex and Rufus each offered a regal paw.

Gemma was confused. How were they going to talk if he whisked himself away now? 'I thought you might stay for supper,' she said in a faltering voice.

'As I say, I've phone calls to make.' His voice was brisk, decisive. He moved toward the door. 'Goodbye, girls...Gemma.'

What did he mean, goodbye? It sounded so final, a brush-off. Gemma sucked in a frightened breath and got to her feet. 'I'll see you out.' The girls began standing up. 'No,' she said sharply. 'You stay here. I want a word with Dr Sam.'

She followed him out to the hall. He strode quickly to the front door, opened it and stepped out into the porch.

Gemma fought for breath and words. 'Sam…' She reached out and touched his arm.

'I'll be back at nine,' he said, 'after Daisy's in bed. We'll talk then. It's up to you whether you tell her that I'm coming.' His voice and eyes were expressionless. He turned and strode down the path.

Stunned, Gemma watched him go. She had never felt so forlorn or bereft in her life.

He arrived dead on nine o'clock. He nodded an acknowledgement of her stumbling greeting, and preceded her down the hall into the sitting room.

Her hands, already cold and clammy with nerves, seemed to get colder. She waved at the drinks tray on a side table. 'Would you—'

'No, thanks, I want a clear head for this.' His eyes bored into hers. Legs wide in a very masculine pose, he stood with his back to the flower-filled fireplace. 'Gemma, do you love me?'

'I…I…'

'Well, do you or don't you? Very straight-forward question. I don't want to hear about your reservations, whether connected to Daisy's feelings or the short time we've known each other. I want to know if you love me.'

Gemma sank down onto the sofa. That was the last question she'd expected. Neither had she expected this almost arrogant attitude. Rather she had thought that he might be a bit on the defensive, angry perhaps but eager to explain himself.

She was holding her breath. 'Yes...' The word came out on a gusty sigh.

Sam nodded. 'Good. Now we've got that out of the way, I'll tell you as briefly and con-cisely as I can why I *deserted*—your word—a young woman nearly ten years ago.' His face looked both grim and sad.

Gemma made a dismissive gesture with her hands. 'Sam, please... I didn't mean...'

'But you did, which means you want an-swers.' He pushed his hands into his trouser pockets.

Gemma stared up at him. 'You mean you *did* desert someone.' She clenched her fists. She didn't want to hear this.

'I had a sort of semi-serious relationship going with a staff nurse. I ditched her when I learned that she was sleeping around with half the hospital. A day or two later she announced that she was pregnant. I was pretty sure the baby, *if* there was one, wasn't mine. She was on the Pill and I was taking precautions.'

'And did you sleep around, Sam?' Her voice was cold.

'No, not when there was something going between Joy and me.'

'I see,' Gemma said thoughtfully, her voice less chilly. 'So, was there a baby?'

'No...though I didn't know that for some time. Joy took herself off, disappeared, rumours circulated. But the possibility that I might have fathered a baby shook me to the core. Made me grow up, turned me into...' he gave a wry smile. '...the mature, sober adult that you see before you. I'd been a bit wild, but not too wild to know that I might have had to accept responsibility for a new life.'

In two strides he crossed the room, sat down on the sofa beside her, and took her hands in his. 'Which is why, my love, you can trust me to care for you and Daisy, because had there been a baby I would have loved and cherished it, as all children should be loved and cherished.'

Wave after wave of relief washed through her. He wasn't perfect, but he was the man she'd thought him to be, a man to be trusted, depended upon. She drew her hands from his and slid them up round his neck. 'Oh, Sam, I do love you,' she murmured.

'The feeling's mutual,' he said, gathering her into his arms.

He left half an hour later. 'Like I told the girls, I do have phone calls to make,' he said, adding, 'by the way, Mother has asked me to pass on an invitation to you and Daisy to come to tea next Sunday. She thinks it's time you met the family. It's one of our regular get-togethers.'

'But...we don't know them,' she faltered.

Sam grinned. 'Precisely—the idea is that after Sunday you will.' He touched her cheek. 'You must come. Daisy will love it, meeting all my nieces and nephews.'

She experienced a moment of panic. 'Have you told your mother about us? Was tea your idea?'

The lopsided grin that turned her insides to marshmallow tipped the corner of his mouth.

'No, love, I haven't told her, but I have a hunch she knows. Very perceptive, my mother. And tea was her own idea.'

She smiled. 'OK, then, if Daisy's happy about it, we'll come.'

CHAPTER TEN

GEMMA saw little of Sam over the next few days. Her list, already packed, continued to lengthen as the pollen count rose and the need for antihistamine injections grew with it.

As for Sam, his house calls doubled as the tummy bug, in the mysterious way that bugs did, made a return visit to Blaney St Mary and the surrounding villages. This had a ripple effect on the surgery, and Helen Brodie, standing in for Ellie, was kept busy answering the phone and making appointments.

On Thursday evening, Sam sandwiched in a brief visit to the cottage between calls. He arrived as Gemma was coming down the stairs, and she saw his silhouette through the coloured glass of the door panels.

She put her finger to her lips as she opened the door. 'Daisy's only just settling,' she murmured. 'If she hears you come in she'll be down like a shot.'

Sam grinned and nodded. 'Sounds as if she'd be pleased to see me.' He followed her into the sitting room. 'And are you pleased to see me?' he asked, swinging her round into his arms. He didn't wait for an answer, but lowered his head and showered darting kisses on her upturned face. Eyes, nose, cheeks, neck and finally mouth. He teased apart her lips with his tongue and explored the moist softness within.

Gemma strained against him, soft breasts to hard chest, and kissed him back, fiercely, hungrily. Her hands cupped the back of his head, locking his face to hers till they were breathing each other's breath.

The insistent burring of Sam's mobile in his top pocket shattered the blissful moment.

He groaned and lifted his head, forcing it back against the pressure of Gemma's hands. He was breathing heavily, deep, rasping breaths as he fumbled in his pocket for the phone. 'Love you,' he muttered as he switched it on. 'Dr Sam,' he said briskly, and listened with a frown to what was being said at the other end.

The voice was shrill and frightened—a child's voice? Gemma got her own breathing under control and eased herself out of the arm that still encircled her.

The voice trailed off into sobs.

Sam said with quiet authority, 'Heather, listen to me. Don't try to get her up from the floor, but roll her onto her left side, making sure her head is turned, and put a cushion at her back so that she won't roll over. Then hold her hands and talk to her. I'll be with you in a few minutes.'

He switched off and smiled a small rueful smile. 'Sorry, Gemma, love, must scoot. One of my young single mums in trouble, sounds as if she might be fitting. Apparently, she's twitching and unrousable. She's not been very well lately, has a slight heart problem due to rheumatic fever as a child, but there was nothing I could pinpoint. This may give me a lead.'

While he'd been speaking he'd moved towards the door and into the hall. Gemma followed him. 'That was her eight-year-old daughter, Heather, phoning. Nice, sensible kid. I've known her since she was a baby. She was my first home delivery when I joined the practice. Against all the odds, Stella's made a super job of bringing her up on her own.'

They reached the front door and he bent and gave her a quick abstracted kiss on the cheek, but his mind wasn't on it. Gemma guessed that it was already with his patient. 'See you to-morrow at the surgery, love,' he said as he strode down the path.

'Hope all goes well,' Gemma called, as he reached the gate.

'Thanks.' He didn't look back, but waved his hand as he slid into his car. Seconds later, he pulled swiftly away.

Gemma watched as he circled the green and headed north out of the village. Her heart went out to the young mother and the little girl, Heather. One of her recurring nightmares was what would happen to Daisy if she herself was taken ill. How would she cope? Who would she call on for help? In a medical emergency, of course, she could phone the surgery, just as young Heather had done, no problem...

But in the long term and if she died...?

There was only Neil, unpredictable and un-reliable, unfit to take custody of Daisy full time. And, of course, her own parents, but which one? Neither knew Daisy, both had part-ners who might resent the intrusion of a small girl into their lives. On the other hand, they might do battle over who should care for her, using her as another tool to hurt each other.

She shuddered at the thought of Daisy going to either of them, or to Neil.

That left Emma, her best friend and Daisy's godmother. But at this moment in time she was nursing in a remote corner of India, and letters took for ever to reach her. In any case, in a year's time she might be in Africa or any other trouble spot in the world where the charity she worked for might send her. No, Emma was a non-starter. The most she could do was offer support from afar.

At least, Gemma thought, staring unseeingly at the television screen, financial security was less of a problem now. The cottage could be sold and the proceeds used to secure Daisy's future in practical terms. She drew in a deep, painful breath. But money didn't buy love, and love was what Daisy would need if anything happened to her. And who would be prepared to give her that?

Sam, of course, shouted a voice in her head. He's already said that he wants to love and care for Daisy. But that's when we're married, cut in a panicky, doubting thought. The voice was scathing. And you think that he would turn his back on her if something happened to you and you weren't married? Get real, woman. He's a man in a million who would cherish Daisy as if she were his own.

And Daisy has already said that she likes him, the voice reminded Gemma—right from his first visit. On the kite outing, other visits, he's always brought a touch of magic with him... There's already a rapport between them. So tell Daisy that he wants to marry you, give her a chance to tell you how she feels. But we've known him for such a short while, hardly time for her to...

What's time got to do with it? A few weeks is a lifetime to a child. Daisy probably feels that she's known him for ever. She's always talking about 'Dr Sam this' and 'Dr Sam that', isn't she?

True! Gemma got up and switched off the television, and turned and stared at herself in the mirror over the fireplace. 'Right,' she told her reflection sternly, 'I shall talk to her to-morrow directly we get home from school, and be totally honest with her about how Sam and I feel about each other, and ask her straight out how she feels about Sam as a stepfather.'

Supposing she's dead against the idea, wondered her treacherous thoughts. Her stomach churned sickeningly at the thought, but her resolve remained firm and, metaphorically squaring her shoulders, she took herself off to bed.

She dreamed about a small girl—not Daisy—drowning, and being plucked from the water by Sam. Tanned, tall, lean and muscular. he bent over her and began resuscitating her on a sandy tropical beach. His face was fierce, intense, as he worked on the fragile little body, a lock of blond hair falling over his forehead.

Abruptly the dream ended and Gemma woke up. Had the little girl been saved...or hadn't she? And did she represent the child, Heather? She couldn't wait to get to work to find out from Sam what had happened to Heather and her mother.

Ellie was behind the reception desk when Gemma went through to collect her list. She looked pale, but otherwise much her usual self, bright-eyed, smiling, calm and collected.

In fact, thought Gemma, there was an aura about her. She was looking quietly radiant, and smiling a Mona Lisa, enigmatic-type smile.

'It's good to see you, Ellie, and, considering what you've been through with that abscess, you look great.'

'I feel it. The antibiotics worked brilliantly, and…' Ellie thrust a list and pile of records toward her. She gave an un-Ellie-like giggle, leaned across the desk, and whispered, 'I'm pregnant. Only a few weeks, but I've tested and I'm positive.' Her pale cheeks flushed. 'Oh, Gemma, I can't believe it after all this time. I'm so happy, and Dave's over the moon. He's actually going to take me out for lunch, and he hasn't done that for yonks.'

Holding back all the cautionary warnings that she felt she should make about it being early days, Gemma said, 'Oh, Ellie, that's wonderful news. I'm so pleased for you. You must tell me more later.' She reached across and gave Ellie a kiss on her cheek. 'But I've got to dash right now. I must see Sam before I start, if he's free.'

'His last patient's just gone. You can catch him before he buzzes for his next one.'

'Thanks.'

Gemma made for his office and knocked on the door. He called to her to come in. He was busy at his monitor, and didn't look round as she slipped into the room.

Her breath caught in her throat. Looking at him, her heart felt as if it were being squeezed tight, her insides melted. He looked so like the man in her dream, bending over the fragile body of the little girl, as then a lock of fair hair falling over his forehead as he peered at the screen.

In a low, husky voice, she said, 'Sam, I don't want to bother you but…'

He swivelled round in his chair and beamed a lopsided smile at her. '*You* could never bother me, Gemma. What about a good-morning kiss?' He opened his arms wide.

She shook her head. 'No fear, I'm staying right here. Someone might come in.'

His eyes gleamed wickedly. 'Not without knocking, and I can always tell them to go away.'

Resisting the temptation to throw herself into his arms, Gemma laughed and kissing the tips of her fingers, blew the air toward him. 'There's your kiss. That's all you're going to get this morning, so make the most of it.'

He heaved a theatrical sigh and let his arms fall to his sides. 'You're a hard woman, Nurse Fellows. So, if you're not here to give me a proper kiss, what brings you to my office?'

'Stella—the emergency you were called out to last night. Her little girl Heather phoned. I haven't been able to get them out of my mind.'

The wicked glint faded, and his eyes suddenly filled with compassion. He said gently. 'I can imagine, a single mum, a small daughter, like you and Daisy. Is that the comparison you were making?'

'Something like that.' No way did she want to tell him in detail the thoughts it had triggered off. 'Please, tell me what happened. Did you have to send her to hospital?'

'No. She was conscious when I arrived, almost back to normal. Don't think it was a true epileptic fit, more a Stokes-Adams syndrome episode. I'm going to arrange for her to have some more cardiac investigations. Could be that she's a suitable candidate for a pacemaker.'

'And Heather. Did you leave her there alone in the house, a little girl trying to look after her mother?' She tried, unsuccessfully, to keep the tone of accusation out of her voice.

'No, love,' Sam said drily, raising a surprised eyebrow. 'You don't really think I'd do that, do you? I arranged for the woman next door, who is a good friend and neighbour, to stay the night with them.'

Gemma's cheeks reddened. 'No,' she whispered, 'I didn't really think you would leave them high and dry to manage for themselves. I don't know why I said that. I'm so sorry. It's just that I couldn't stop thinking about them…'

'And if something like that could happen to you and Daisy?'

She nodded.

He crossed the room and took her in his arms. 'Not,' he said, 'whilst I've breath in my body. If anything happened to you, love, I would take care of Daisy.' He kissed the top of her head. 'OK?'

'OK,' she quavered.

The rest of the day passed in a flash. The usual mixture of patients came and went. She took blood, gave injections, applied dressings, cleaned and stitched wounds and reassured. Always there was a need for reassurance. Just, she thought dreamily, a warm glow spreading inside her, as Sam had reassured *her*.

She wrenched her thoughts away from Sam, and concentrated on the job in hand, the redressing of a particularly unpleasant varicose ulcer that was slow to heal.

'Come back in five days, Mrs Snow,' she told the patient. 'If it's not improving, I'll talk to one of the doctors about trying a new treatment.'

She looked at her watch after Mrs Snow had gone—ten to three, time to clear up before fetching Daisy from school.

Fetch Daisy from school and... Her stomach clenched, she felt breathless, nauseated... She was going to ask her small daughter the most important question in her young life. There was no way of softening or embroidering it. When it came down to it, the question was— would she or wouldn't she accept Sam as her stepfather?

It began to rain as Gemma and Daisy started up the green. It had been raining on and off all day, short, sharp showers from dark clouds interspersed with brilliant blue skies.

'April showers,' said Gemma, opening up her yellow umbrella, bright with red poppies, and cuddling Daisy to her side so that they were both protected from the darting rain.

'But it's May,' protested Daisy, at her most pragmatic, 'so it's May showers.'

Gemma laughed down at the dear little up-turned face. 'OK, poppet, I concede. It's May showers.'

'What's concede?'

'To give in,' Gemma explained as they reached the cottage.

They left their wet macs in the hall and went straight through to the kitchen, warmed on this rain-chilled spring afternoon by the elderly but functional Aga.

'I've got a treat as it's Friday,' said Gemma, going to the fridge and removing a large bag. She held it aloft. 'Cream chocolate doughnuts and, drinkwise, you can name your poison, love—Coke, limeade, lemonade?'

Daisy clapped her hands. 'Cream dough-nuts, yummy, and I'll have Coke, please, Mummy.' She giggled. 'It rhymes—Mummy, yummy.'

Gemma felt a little catch in her throat. She thought, She's always extra bubbly on Fridays, on account of us spending the weekend to-gether and planning what we're going to do. So what about this Friday? This Friday which will alter our whole lives? This Friday that will mark the beginning, the end, or at least might put a hold on, my relationship with Sam.

She tried to squash the nausea that gripped her stomach as she poured the Coke. Some splashed on the table.

'Mummy, why are your hands all shaky?' Daisy asked.

Gemma sat down at the opposite side of the table with a loud bump and took in a long, deep breath. She produced a smile of sorts. 'Because, Daisy, love, I have something to tell you, and I don't know how to begin, how to explain. I just want you to know that I love you more than anyone in the world, and I want you to be happy—I want us to be happy together, always.' Her voice came out as if she had a cold.

Daisy, her mouth ringed with cream, about to take a second bite of her doughnut, stared at Gemma, and her eyes were suddenly filled with tears, which brimmed over and trickled down her cheeks.

'Mummy, don't die, please, don't die.'

Gemma knocked her chair over in her haste to get round the table. She knelt beside Daisy and folded her in her arms, hugging her tight and kissing her wet cheeks.

'Darling, I'm not going to die,' she murmured between kisses. 'Oh, baby, whatever made you think that?' She rocked her backwards and forwards.

Daisy heaved in a sobbing, trembling breath. 'You sound so funny, as if you want to tell me something bad, something that will hurt.' She blinked at Gemma through her tears and scrubbed at her eyes with balled-up fists. 'Are you sure you're not going to die, or go away and leave me? Promise you're not going to, Mummy, promise me!'

Gemma hugged her even tighter. 'Darling, I promise. I'm as fit as a fiddle, I'm not going to die. And *I* don't think what I have to tell you is bad, and I hope it won't hurt you. But it will surprise you and I want you to think about what I have to say very carefully. There's no rush and you can ask me anything you want. Will you do that, sweetheart?'

Daisy lifted her head, which had been buried in Gemma's neck, and stared her straight in the face for a moment, her green, tear-filled eyes unwavering.

'It sounds very important,' she said in a whispery voice.

'It is, love, it's something that will change our whole lives.'

'We don't have to go back and live in London, do we?' Daisy's voice rose to a squeak. 'I'd hate that. I want to live here always, in the village with Katy, and I want you to work at the surgery with Dr Sam and everyone, and be happy...' Her voice trailed off.

Gemma's heart jumped at her mention of Sam. It was like an omen, it had to be her cue. All she had to do was pick the right words. Keep it simple, her instincts told her.

She cupped Daisy's tear-stained face in her hands and kissed her on her nose. 'I want all those things too,' she said softly, 'and so does Dr Sam. He doesn't want us to go away, ever. He has asked me to marry him, but I said I would have to ask you first.'

She fought to keep calm, but her heartbeats hammered against her chest wall and thundered in her ears.

All sorts of expressions flitted across Daisy's face, ending with a frown. 'Will Dr Sam be my daddy if you marry him?'

'He'll be your stepfather. Daddy will remain Daddy, he's your natural father.' Please, don't let her ask what natural means, not now. I'll explain it some time.

'Will Daddy still come to visit?'

'Yes.' Don't enlarge upon it, she warned herself. This was going to be a long session. Her knees were numb. She dropped her hands from Daisy's face, dragged a chair round the table next to Daisy's and shifted onto it.

Daisy looked thoughtful. 'Will Dr—? Oh, I won't be able to him call him Dr Sam when you're married, will I? What will I call him?'

Gemma thought she might faint, though she'd never fainted in her life. Did this mean what she thought it meant? She cleared her throat. 'Do you mean that you think I *should* marry Dr Sam?' she asked, trying desperately to sound matter-of-fact.

Daisy pursed her rosy lips and nodded, slowly bouncing her reddish-brown curls. Her pursed lips curved into a smile. 'Yes,' she said at last. 'I think it would be brilliant if you did... I like Dr Sam. In fact, I think I love him. I'm glad he's going to be my stepfather.' She looked at Gemma thoughtfully. 'So, what do you think I should call him, Mummy?'

Gemma, dizzy with happiness, hardly able to take in the fact that Daisy actually wanted her to marry Sam, unable to think straight, smiled at her through eyes misty with tears. 'I don't know, love,' she said tremulously. 'I think we'd better ask him.'

The conversation for the rest of the evening was mostly about the wedding. Daisy wanted answers. When would it be? Could she be a bridesmaid? Gemma, making a terrific effort to concentrate, explained that it wouldn't be for a while yet, that she and Sam had a lot to talk about and there was much to be arranged, but, yes, of course, she would be a bridesmaid. They talked colours and styles of dresses and all the fairy-tale things that small girls associated with weddings.

Gemma, weak with relief and happiness, romanticised with her. She had no idea what sort of a wedding Sam envisaged, but somehow they would fit in all Daisy's ideas of what it should be.

Bubbling over, Daisy wanted to know if she could ring Katy and tell her that Mummy was going to marry Dr Sam. Not for the moment, Gemma explained. Sam hadn't yet told Dr Mallory or Mrs M. that they were going to get married.

'We wanted you to be the first to know,' she added, 'because you are the most important person in our lives. I know it's hard for you to keep a secret from your best friend, but just this once, love, you must.'

'When do you think Dr Sam will tell Dr Mallory and Mrs M.?' Daisy asked.

Gemma smiled and kissed her small nose. 'Just as soon as I let him know that we have your blessing, poppet.'

'Oh, have I given you my blessing?' asked Daisy.

'Yes, love, that's exactly what you've done.'

Daisy gave a huge sigh and yawned. 'I'm glad,' she said. 'It sounds nice, a blessing. Now I think I'd better go to bed. I'm pooped.' She gave a little chuckly laugh. 'That's what Katy's granny says when she's tired— pooped.'

Gemma phoned Sam as soon as soon as Daisy was tucked up in bed and fast asleep. He was on call till midnight when Bob Carstairs would relieve him, but she caught him between patients.

She said breathlessly, as soon as he answered, 'I've told Daisy.'

He whistled in a breath through his teeth. 'And...?' His usual clear tenor sounded gravelly.

'She's over the moon, thrilled to bits, can't wait for us to get married.'

She heard him take in another deep breath. 'Hallelujah. Thank God for that. I was so afraid…'

'So was I, but you said all would be well and that's how it's turned out.'

'I'll be over.'

'But you're on call.'

'So? My mobile works as well in your house as in mine.' He clicked off.

He arrived a few minutes later, and gathered her in his arms as soon as he was in the hall. He gave her a hard, long kiss, not particularly sexy but very satisfying, a married sort of kiss, she thought. Without warning, he swept her up in his arms carried her into the sitting room.

'Happy?' he asked in a low, throaty voice as he lowered her to the floor.

'Unbelievably. I feel as if a huge weight has been lifted from my shoulders. Oh, Sam, I can't tell you how deep-down scared I've been, wondering how to tell Daisy, dreading that she would hate the idea of us getting married, and wondering what we would do if she did.'

She sagged suddenly against him. 'I'm pooped,' she said with a rather hysterical giggle. She looked up into his gently smiling face. 'That's what Katy's granny says when she's tired,' she explained solemnly.

Sam tightened his hold round her and sank down onto the sofa, cuddling her to him. He rocked her to and fro like a baby. 'You're emotionally exhausted, dear heart,' he said softly. 'You must go to bed and have a good night's sleep.'

'I like it when you call me dear heart,' she murmured, snuggling against his chest. 'It makes me feel safe and...'

'Cherished!'

She smiled sleepily. 'Yes, that's the word. I don't think I've ever been cherished before.'

'Then prepare yourself for a lot of cherishing in the future, but right now it's off to bed with you.' As if to endorse his words, his mobile chirped into life. He kissed her forehead and pushed her off his lap. 'Go on—bed,' he said sternly, steering her towards the door. 'I'll let myself out.' He clicked on the switch.

'Dr Sam,' she heard him say as she made her way up the stairs, pausing halfway up to blow him a tired hit-or-miss kiss.

He grinned, a lopsided, loving grin. 'Good-night,' he mouthed. 'Sleep tight.'

She did. She fell into bed and remembered nothing else till the morning.

Saturday passed as most Saturdays did, in a welter of small routine activities. Though she missed him dreadfully, Gemma was rather glad that she wasn't seeing anything of Sam that day. He had surgery in the morning and a GP meeting in Bournemouth, spanning the after-noon and evening.

It was a good opportunity, she thought, to keep everything as normal as possible, as if nothing momentous had happened to alter their lives. So she and Daisy went swimming and shopping in Shillingbourne as usual, but plans for the future kept popping into the conversa-tion and they were both on a high.

Daisy kept up an endless stream of chatter. The matter of what she should call Sam when he became her stepfather was still top of her agenda. 'I shall ask him tomorrow,' she de-cided, 'at the tea-party.'

'Perhaps,' Gemma suggested, 'it would be better for the three of us to sit down together and talk this over in private. There will be a lot of people there and they might not all know that Sam and I are getting married. He might only have told Dr Mallory and Mrs M.'

She couldn't have been more wrong. The whole family had been put in the picture by the time she and Daisy arrived at the manor house.

Sam greeted them with the news as he threw open the massive iron-studded front door and welcomed them into the timbered hall.

His eyes met Gemma's over Daisy's head. 'Sorry, I've rather jumped the gun. I just couldn't wait to tell everyone about us,' he said, pulling a rueful face. 'Don't be mad at me.'

Before she could answer, Daisy said in her practical little voice, 'Mummy won't be mad at you, 'cause she loves you.'

Sam crouched down so that his twinkling eyes were on a level with hers. 'Are you sure about that, Daisy?'

Daisy nodded. 'Oh, yes, pos'tive.'

Sam smiled. 'May I give you a kiss?' he asked softly.

'Because you're going to be my stepfather?'

'That, and to thank you for being prepared to share Mummy with me.'

Daisy dimpled. 'And because I gave you my blessing?'

Sam grinned. 'Got it in one,' he said.

Daisy offered a rosy cheek. 'Just here,' she said, pointing to a spot in the middle.

Sam gave her a loud, smacking kiss.

'And this one.' She offered the other cheek and he repeated the kiss.

'Now, let's go and meet everyone,' he said, taking each of them by the hand and leading them across the gleaming oak floor towards one of the heavy wooden doors opening off the hall. They could hear laughter and the sound of voices as they approached.

Gemma stopped as they reached the door, and took a deep breath. 'I'm scared,' she murmured. 'You've got such a big family, we've got no one.'

Sam kissed her cheek noisily as he had Daisy's. 'My family is your family,' he said softly, 'and they're all dying to meet you both.'

Sam was right. It was obvious that his brother, Luke, and his sisters, Mattie and Ann, and their respective partners, Jane, Mark and

Simon, were eager to welcome them. They weren't in the least bit fazed by the fact that Sam was proposing to marry someone whom he'd only known for a few weeks. Everyone seemed to think it was a brilliant idea.

'It was the same with Mark and me,' Mattie confided to Gemma. 'A case of love at first sight. We got hitched six weeks after we met. The parents were thrilled to bits. But, then, that's how it was for them, too. They clapped eyes on each other for the first time over an anaesthetised patient in Theatre, and, bingo, that was it. They wanted to be together and got married in no time flat. They have a thing about togetherness.'

That was true if the rest of the afternoon was anything to go by. Everyone went out of their way to make Gemma feel wanted, close.

And Daisy was having a wonderful time with the other children. After tea, Nicola, Paul, Fliss and Tom, with two-year-old Lucy clutching Daisy's hand, all trooped out to the orchard to play. Mrs M. and Dr Mallory, humping his year-old grandson Frank on his broad shoulders, went along to supervise them.

Gemma guessed that it was a diplomatic move to give the younger members of the family a chance to talk amongst themselves, four pairs of people with much in common. She heaved a sigh of pure pleasure as for the first time in many years, she basked in the delight of being one of a pair and part of a family.

The party broke up at seven. Tired children were reunited with their parents and deposited in various cars parked on the drive. Goodbye and thank-you kisses were exchanged, promises made to phone, and repeat congratulations called to Sam and Gemma.

Gemma turned to Mrs M. and Dr Mallory as the last of the cars disappeared down the drive. 'We must go now,' she said, holding out her hand. 'Thank you for a lovely party and making us feel so welcome. You have an absolutely super family.'

'And you're part of it now,' replied Mrs M., ignoring Gemma's hand and giving her a hug and a kiss. She bent down and kissed the top of Daisy's head. 'And you've brought us another grandchild.'

Dr Mallory kissed them both too. His blue eyes twinkled as Sam's did. 'Nice to have you in the family firm as well as the medical one,' he said to Gemma, his voice rather gruff.

'Could have predicted this the day you joined us.'

Gemma looked startled. 'How?'

He tapped his finger to his nose. 'Intuition, my dear. Women don't have the monopoly, you know, and if I thought you were a cracker, I knew damn fine that Sam would, too.'

CHAPTER ELEVEN

THE days following the party flew by, happy, busy days for all of them. The news of the engagement spread like wildfire, and all the village showered Sam and Gemma with good wishes.

Gemma told Ellie early on Monday morning, wanting her to be the first to know outside the family. And Daisy was given permission to tell Katy of the engagement.

Secure in the knowledge that she was pregnant, Ellie was beside herself with delight. 'You and Sam are so right for each other,' she said, giving Gemma a hug. 'And how perfect for Daisy to have a man like him for a father. He's a very special sort of person and will love her as if she were his own.'

'I know,' replied Gemma, hugging her back. 'He thinks the world of her, and she adores him. Oh, Ellie, I can't believe this is happening to us. Everything I could ever have hoped for has come true since we arrived in Blaney St Mary. It's the magic of the place.'

'You brought the magic with you,' said Ellie, misty eyed. 'I've got pregnant and you've got Sam.'

It was eleven-thirty on the following Thursday morning when the comparative peace of the surgery, with its steady hum of conversation from the waiting patients, was suddenly shattered.

From the car park in front of the building came the unmistakable sound of a vehicle hitting a solid object, metal crumpling against stone.

Dr Mallory and Sam emerged from their consulting rooms at one end of the corridor as Gemma erupted, almost at a run, from the treatment room at the other end. Ellie, at the reception desk, had a head start, but Gemma and Sam overtook her and were first through the main door.

A low-slung red car was straddling the pavement, with its long nose buried in the cobbled wall fronting the car park. Slewed round in the mouth of the car park was a Land Rover. Sam realised, as he and Gemma sidled round it to reach the damaged car, that it belonged to Steve Smith, the patient he had just examined.

Steve was climbing out of the Land Rover, looking pale and shaken. 'Weren't my fault. Bloody fool was turning in too fast—almost ran into me!' he shouted loudly with a quiver in his voice.

Sam called firmly, 'It's OK, Steve. Stay there, sit on the wall and take a few deep breaths.'

The driver of the sports car was slumped over the steering-wheel, his head resting against the cracked but unbroken laminated window.

Sam opened the driver's door. 'The idiot isn't wearing a seat belt,' he ground out under his breath. 'May have a whiplash or worse.'

Dr Mallory and Ellie arrived.

'Anything I can do, Sam?' Dr Mallory asked briskly.

'Take a look at Steve Smith. He's a bit shocked and not too brilliant. Been having some trouble with his angina and this hasn't helped. You go, too, Ellie. Gemma and I can manage here.'

'Will do.' Dr Mallory strode away to where Steve was sitting on the wall. Ellie followed him.

Gemma stared at the car, suddenly realising how familiar it was. She felt the blood leave her cheeks. 'Oh God it's Neil,' she whispered, pushing past Sam and crouching down to peer up into the driver's face. 'Neil, can you hear me?'

Neil groaned and tried to lift his head.

'Don't move suddenly, old chap,' said Sam sharply, placing the palm of his hand lightly on Neil's head. 'You may have hurt your neck. Stay put for a moment.' He touched Gemma's shoulder. 'Gemma, we need a support collar and my emergency bag,' he said gently but urgently. 'Will you fetch them, please?'

Gemma looked up and nodded. She rose a little unsteadily to her feet. Years of training and of dealing with crises came to her aid. 'Of course,' she said in a small but firm voice. 'Anything else?'

'Take Ellie with you and get her to phone for an ambulance. Report possible whiplash and/or head injury, and let them know that there might be other injuries. Then she can phone Mum and ask her to come over. And she can make an announcement to the patients to the effect that we'll all be running a bit late.'

It was reassuring to be given orders in his calm, authoritative voice, and a relief to be doing something constructive. Gemma relayed the messages to Ellie who was helping Dr Mallory support Steve Smith back to the surgery.

Her mind was in overdrive as she collected the bag and a collar and sped back to the car. Her emotions were mixed. She was shocked and anxious about Neil, and prayed that he wasn't badly injured, but she was angry, too. How typical of him to be driving without a seat belt. Would he never grow up? Now that the initial shock was over, she was astonished at how curiously detached she felt, as if the driver of the car was a stranger, not her ex-husband.

Now if it had been Sam... Hissing an expletive through clenched teeth, she clamped down on the thought.

Sam was still bent over at an awkward angle, supporting Neil's head and talking to him in a low voice, when she reached the car.

He glanced Gemma a quick, reassuring smile. 'You get in the passenger seat and fix the collar, love, while I ease his head up.'

Very gently, with one hand on Neil's forehead and the other steadying the crown of his head, Sam tilted him back, enabling Gemma to fit the collar beneath Neil's chin and round his neck, keeping his head in alignment with his spine.

'That more comfortable, Neil?' Sam asked when they'd finished.

'Mmm,' Neil slurred. Had he heard? Was he answering the question? Gemma kept her eyes glued on his face, willing him to full consciousness.

Sam looked across at her. He seemed to have homed in on her thoughts. 'If you can find me the ophthalmoscope, love, I'll examine his eyes. Might give us a clue to what's happening.'

Gemma said. 'Oh, yes, of course,' in an abstracted voice. She fumbled in the emergency bag and found the instrument.

Sam took it from her and bent over Neil. Carefully he parted his eyelids. 'Hmm, pupils are equal and there's normal dilation,' he grunted after a moment. He touched Neil's face. 'Come, on old chap, time to wake up,' he said in a clear, firm voice.

Neil muttered something and his eyelids fluttered a couple of times and then remained open. He frowned. 'Where the devil...? Oh, yes—hit the wall.' A look of panic came into his eyes. 'Can't move,' he mumbled.

'You're not supposed to,' said Gemma softly. 'You've got a neck brace on in case you've sustained a whiplash injury.'

'Right,' breathed Neil through gritted teeth. He was ashen. 'But it's my bloody leg that's giving me hell.'

Gemma heaved a sigh of relief. Thank God he was conscious and fully alert.

'Which leg?' asked Sam.

'The right, my knee feels as if it's busted.' His voice cracked, his face was contorted with pain.

Gemma took his hand and squeezed it. 'Hang in there,' she murmured softly.

'OK, I'll take a look at it as well as I can,' said Sam, 'but I don't want to move you until the ambulance arrives, because of a possible neck injury, so I'll have to examine it on the spot. Pain anywhere else—chest, stomach, arms?'

'Nothing to speak of,' Neil slurred, his teeth still clenched together.

'I'll have to cut your trouser leg off above the knee.' Sam crouched down to bring himself level with the injured limb.

'Christ, what does that matter?' Neil mouthed thickly. 'Just get on with it.'

Gemma handed Sam scissors from the bag. He nodded his thanks and began snipping away the expensive material. The cut-off trousers revealed a hugely swollen, grossly inflamed and distorted knee.

Sam crouched down on his haunches and examined the joint with careful, sensitive fingers.

'Not surprised you're in a lot of pain,' he said. 'Your knee's badly dislocated, and there might be a fracture concealed by the dislocation. It's a hospital job. Needs an orthopaedic surgeon to tackle it and it'll have to be X-rayed to determine whether there is a fracture and the dislocation needs to be reduced under anaesthetic. But I can give you something for the pain—that'll help a bit. Draw me up 50mgs of pethidine, please, Gemma.'

As if on cue, the ambulance was heard approaching as Sam injected the painkilling drug. 'It works quite quickly—should hold you till you get to hospital,' he said kindly.

Neil grunted out a feeble acknowledgement, but his eyes sought out Gemma's. 'Come with me, Gem,' he mumbled.

She managed a smile. 'Just try to stop me,' she said, stroking his forehead and just touching his cheek with her lips. It was a cool, distant kiss of comfort. I ought to be feeling more than this professional compassion, she thought, but I can't.

The transfer to the ambulance by the skilled crew took only a few minutes.

Sam took her hand briefly as his eyes met hers for an instant. 'Take care,' he said softly. 'I'm only at the end of the phone.'

'Thank you.' Her eyes tried to tell him how much she loved him. 'I'll try to get back in time to collect Daisy from school.'

Sam's eyes conveyed their own message of love. 'Don't worry about it,' he said. 'I'll collect her. And tell Neil not to worry about the car. I'll take care of everything.'

And he would, thought Gemma as she climbed into the ambulance, her heart bursting with pride at the thought of his capacity to care. He was, as Ellie had said, a very special sort of man.

*　　*　　*

The church clock struck six as Gemma got out of the taxi in front of Cherry Tree Cottage. She heaved a huge sigh as it drove off. How good it was to be home. She felt as if she had been away for days instead of hours. Hours spent talking to Neil, every moment of which had emphasised the chasm between his upbeat life-style and hers. It seemed incredible that they had once been husband and wife, and that he, Peter Pan character that he was, was her sensible little Daisy's father.

Bone- and mind-weary from the emotional and physical stresses of the day, she heaved another sigh. She wanted a drink and something to eat, but most of all she ached to see Daisy and Sam.

They should be coming any minute if Sam had timed it right from the phone call she had made to say she was leaving the hospital. Shielding her eyes from the summer evening sun, she looked across the green. And there they were, running towards her, hand in hand, Daisy's little legs going like pistons to keep up with Sam's long strides which he was slowing to accommodate hers.

Daisy flung herself into Gemma's arms, her chubby little face screwed up with anxiety.

'How's Daddy?' she panted. 'Is he going to be all right?'

Gemma hugged her tight. 'He'll be fine, love. He had a lot of X-rays which showed that he hasn't broken any bones. But he's hurt his leg and it's bandaged up and he'll have to walk with crutches for a bit, but otherwise he's OK. He sends you his love and a big kiss.'

He hadn't, he was feeling too sorry himself, but Daisy needn't know that. It was a necessary little white lie.

'Will he have to stay in hospital?'

'No, he's going to stay with friends. They came to fetch him while I was still at the hospital. That's one of the reasons I've been rather a long time, waiting for them to come.' She smiled lovingly at Sam over Daisy's head. There was so much she wanted to tell him.

His eyes were brimming over with tenderness. He said softly, 'You look whacked, love. You've had a long, worrying day—you need a stiff G and T.' He steered them up the garden path, relieved Gemma of her shoulder bag and found the key.

'I've had a long day, too,' said Daisy, as he ushered them into the hall. 'I think I need a G and T.'

Drunk with tiredness, Gemma leaned against Sam and laughed helplessly. It was a typical Daisy remark.

Sam chuckled. 'You can have a C and L,' he said, as unceremoniously, to Daisy's delight, he swept Gemma up into his arms, carried her through to the sitting room and dumped her on the sofa.

'Thanks,' she murmured, and, sinking back against the cushions, closed her eyes and listened through a haze of exhaustion to the conversation between Sam and Daisy.

'What's a C and L?' asked Daisy.

'Coke and lemonade with chunks of ice in it—scrumptious. You fetch the bottles and the ice from the kitchen and I'll mix the drinks.'

Daisy sped off to the kitchen, bustling back a few minutes later with the bottles and ice precariously balanced on a tray.

Sam smartly took the tray from her.

'Wow,' she said, her eyes shining. 'I've never had Coke *and* lemonade before.'

'Special occasion,' replied Sam.

'Why's it special, because of Daddy not having to stay in hospital?'

'That, and because tonight Mummy and I are going to fix the date of our wedding. I think it ought to be soon, don't you, poppet? Like we said this afternoon, the sooner the better.'

Gemma's eyes flew open. 'What do you mean, fix the date of the wedding?' She looked uncertainly at the two loved faces. 'Sam...I thought we'd decided to wait before fixing anything. We need time, so much to talk about, like where we're going to live...and Daisy needs time...' Her voice trailed off.

Daisy slid off her chair and crossed the room to perch on the side of the sofa. 'No, I don't, Mummy.' Her voice was very earnest. Her straight eyebrows came together in a frown over her neat little nose. She took Gemma's free hand in her two small pudgy ones in an adult, reassuring sort of way. 'I love Sam and you love him too,' she said, 'and I want us to live with him in his house. There's lots of room, it would be like here only bigger, and when I have brothers and sisters we'll need more room, won't we?'

Gemma's mind boggled. What the devil had they been talking about while she'd been sitting by Neil's bedside?

'Out of the mouths of babes and innocents comes devastating logic,' murmured Sam. His eyes twinkled madly, his mouth quirked into his heart-stopping, lopsided smile.

Daisy turned an enquiring face to his. 'What's logic?' she asked.

Sam's eyebrows shot up in surprise. Then he took in a deep breath. 'It's—'

Gemma gave him a warning glance and shook her head. Now was definitely not the time for a philosophical lecture that would lead to further whys and whats. He would soon learn that the questions were endless.

She said quickly, 'I'll explain later, love. Right now...' she put her glass down with a shaky hand '...I think you deserve a hug.' She opened her arms wide.

Daisy scrambled into them. She tilted her head to one side. 'Why do I deserve a hug?'

'Because you are right, both of you.' She included Sam in her smile. 'There's no reason on earth why we shouldn't be married as soon as possible.'

'*Wow!*' Daisy sighed. 'That's scrummy.'

'I second that,' said Sam, crossing the room to perch himself on the arm of the sofa. 'It's a brilliant, very intelligent decision.' He dropped kisses, first on Daisy's head and then on Gemma's. 'Now, how about if I cook us omelettes for supper—a big one for me, medium one for Mummy and a small one for Daisy?'

'Like the three bears,' said Daisy. 'Daddy bear, Mummy bear and Baby bear.'

'That's us,' said Sam.

By eight o'clock, an excited but finally pooped-out Daisy was safely tucked up in bed and Gemma and Sam were seated side by side on the sofa. They were acutely aware of each other, of the warmth and vibes flowing between them and the intense longing to be in each other's arms, yet by unspoken agreement they kept an inch or two of space between them.

There was the matter of Neil and the accident to be sorted out and put into perspective. Gemma knew that his arrival so dramatically on the scene needed to be explained. Sam would have guessed that she and Neil would have talked while they were waiting at the hospital. He had avoided probing whilst Daisy was still around, but he must be itching to know what she and Neil had discussed.

Well, here goes, she thought. She held up her glass of red wine so that evening sun slanted on it, making it glow like a jewel.

She took a sip. 'Funny,' she mused, 'how easily Daisy was reassured about Neil once I explained that he had only minor injuries. I thought she might be more upset. Not that they've exactly got a strong father-daughter relationship. And you'd already briefed her about the accident so she was prepared for what I had to tell her.'

'Yes. I explained what his injuries might be, but kept it low-key. And I had the impression that as long as he wasn't at death's door, she would take it in her stride, as, in fact, she did. But, then, that tallies with being six years old and talking about somebody who plays a very limited role in her life, doesn't it?' There was a curious note in his voice.

'Yes.' Gemma turned to look at him.

He was leaning forward, his elbows on his knees, cradling his glass in both hands and peering down into the ruby red liquid. 'The thing is,' he continued softly, 'although I didn't know your ex-husband, except for the short while that I treated him today, he's played a major, rather than a limited, role in my life.' His fingers tightened round the stem of his glass till his knuckles whitened.

Gemma frowned, a frown which he didn't see because he was still staring into his wine. 'I don't understand what you mean,' she said, wanting to take the glass from his hands and massage the tense fingers.

He turned his head sharply and focused his eyes, dark with pain, on hers. 'What I mean, Gemma—' his voice was thick, low, husky '—is that from the first time I saw him, driving away from the cottage like a maniac, I've been jealous as hell of him, just knowing that he was around somewhere...

'Of course I didn't know then that he was your ex-husband. I saw him kiss you, thought he was someone special to you, and then when he turned up again at the surgery... God help me, I could have killed him. I came to the conclusion that you were still in love with him and were encouraging him back.'

He took a huge gulp of wine. 'And even today, in spite of everything, just for a moment or two I wondered. You were so tender with him, held his hand, kissed him...and then knowing you were together at the hospital all those hours, talking.' He shrugged and dredged up a wry smile. 'Well, let's say I had a job to keep my mind on my work.'

Gemma looked at him with astonished eyes. 'Oh, Sam, how could you think that? If we hadn't been finished years ago, today's accident would have convinced me that I didn't love him. All I could think of when we were treating him, before we knew that he wasn't critically injured, was thank God it wasn't you lying there.'

She drained her wine in one swallow and put her glass down with a shaky hand. 'And if it weren't for Daisy, I would never see him again. Not that we will be seeing so much of him in the future—he's been promoted and he's off to Australia to open up an office in Melbourne. He won't be able to come back from there every five minutes.'

Sam inhaled deeply. 'That,' he said in a deeply satisfied voice, 'is great news. I presume he hared down to see you to boast of his promotion.'

Gemma was surprised by his uncharacteristic sarcasm. 'No, he came because I had written to let him know that we were getting married.'

He frowned and slammed his glass down on the table. 'Did you *have* to write?' His usual cool seemed to have deserted him.

Gemma rested her hand on his arm. 'Sam, it was a courtesy letter on account of Daisy,' she said gently.

'Sorry.' He pulled a face. 'Of course it was, but where he's concerned… Truth is, love, I'm just so scared of losing you, after waiting all these years for you to come along, that I can't see straight.' He picked up her hand and pressed her palm to his lips. 'So, *please*, marry me and put me out of my misery. I'll get a special licence or whatever and we'll nip in to the nearest registry office and do the deed.'

Gemma took hold of both his strong, lean hands and held them prayer-like in her own. 'No, not a registry office, my darling. I don't mind what sort of wedding we have, but Daisy does, and so do your parents. They want you to be married in the village church as they were, with Uncle Tom Cobley and all, and particularly—'

'Old Harry Trotter,' Sam broke in. He grinned his lopsided grin that made her heart flip like a mad thing. 'So be it, a fairy-tale wedding it will be, with all the trimmings.' He pulled her into his arms. 'And to be honest, I'd rather have it this way. Though I'd have married anywhere to please you, to make sure of you.'

He bent forward and planted a kiss on her nose, then freed his hands, which were still clasped between hers, and took her into his arms and onto his lap. 'Because I'm like Dad, I like continuity. I love being part of this small community, knowing my young patients and their parents, and often their grandparents. I couldn't live or work anywhere else. And I want you and Daisy to love it too.'

'Oh, Sam, we already do,' she said firmly. Her green eyes blazed. 'This is where we belong—with you in Blaney St Mary. You're stuck with us for good, I'm afraid.'

He nuzzled the top of her head and trailed kisses over her face and neck, beneath her chin and up to her mouth. She closed her eyes and waited for his kiss, but it didn't come immediately.

She opened her eyes. 'What's wrong?' she whispered.

'Nothing's wrong,' he whispered back. 'I was just feasting my eyes on your dear, lovely face, absorbing the fact that if I cherish you I can feast upon it every day for the rest of my life.'

Gemma said breathlessly, 'You're a romantic old thing, aren't you?'

He wrinkled his nose. 'I'll disregard the "old" and have you know that all Mallory men have a strong romantic streak in them—that, and the virtue of keeping their women. When I say "I do" at the altar...' he raised a questioning eyebrow '...*when*?'

'Six weeks' time, end of June,' Gemma said promptly.

'I promise you, it'll be for keeps.'

EPILOGUE

TIMOTHY and Tara bawled their heads off throughout the baptismal service.

'Good sign that, they be crying out the devil,' sang out Old Harry Trotter from the midst of the congregation in the nave of the church.

Several people nearby shushed him, but the Mallory family, grouped round the ancient font, smiled at each other. It was a typical Harry remark.

Daisy whispered to Katy, who was standing beside her close to the font, 'They must have a lot of devil in them—they cry an awful lot.'

''Spect they'll grow out of it,' Katy whispered back.

'Yes, when the devil's all cried out,' replied Daisy in her pragmatic fashion.

Gemma and Sam, overhearing the whispered exchange, smiled down on them, and then across at their two noisy offspring in the arms of their respective godparents.

Sam clasped Gemma's hand tightly and gave her his special, just-for-her smile. The awareness vibes were bouncing back and forth between them. They were both remembering!

It was a year to the day that they had stood at the altar and made their vows. A June day just like today, with brilliant sunshine pouring through the magnificent stained-glass windows in a mosaic of colour. Lozenges of red, green and blue splashed on the heads of the congregation, on the wooden pews and stone-flagged floors and on the brass urns full of lupins and delphiniums and branches of white, sweet-scented syringa.

The scent of the mock orange blossom had filled the church then as it filled it now, only then it had mingled with the scent of the mimosa and white roses in her bouquet, a bouquet cleverly imitated in Daisy's tiny posy. Just as Daisy's dress had been a replica, except in colour, of Gemma's—Empire-line in style, with tiny puff sleeves, the muslin falling in graceful folds from the high bodice. Daisy's was a soft rose pink, Gemma's a creamy gold.

Gemma's eyes prickled with happy tears. It had been a lovely wedding day. She reached out and lightly touched Daisy's head—it had been her day too.

Daisy turned and glanced her a dimpling grin and took in a deep breath, wrinkling her nose. 'Nice,' she mouthed.

Gemma nodded. Was she associating the scent with the wedding? she wondered.

Sam's hand tightened on hers and she lifted her head as the vicar marked first Timothy's then Tara's small foreheads with water from the font…

'In the name of the Father, the Son and the Holy Ghost, I baptise thee,' he intoned in his strong, carrying voice. 'And now,' he said, 'on this happy day, by special request from Daisy, the twins' sister, we will sing ''All things bright and beautiful''.'

The congregation rose to its collective feet, the organ burst forth and several dozen voices were raised to the ancient beams as they sang their hearts out to the old favourite, Daisy's shrill little treble competing with Sam's vibrant tenor.

It was nearly midnight. Gemma and Sam sat side by side in the huge, canopied four-poster that would have put any modern king-size bed to shame, each feeding a baby. Sam was supplementary bottle-feeding Tara, Gemma breast- feeding Timothy.

The room was dim, lit only by the orange glow from the bedside lamps. And it was quiet, except for an occasional glug from one or other of the sucking babies. Gemma was supporting Timothy, whose rosebud mouth was firmly latched onto her nipple, with one arm resting on a pillow, and with her free hand she was entering the day's events in her diary.

Not having a hand free, Sam had an open book propped up against his hunched-up knees, but he wasn't reading. A dreamy smile on his face, he was watching Gemma and his son.

'I wish I could paint,' he said softly. 'You look exquisite when you're feeding the babies. I'd love to capture the look of you on paper.'

Gemma chuckled her sweet husky laugh. 'You've taken zillions of photos and nearly worn the video camera out,' she murmured, leaning over to brush his night-bearded cheek with her lips.

'Not the same,' he said. 'I want to *taste* you.'

'Be my guest.' She laughed, tilting her head so that the lightly tanned column of her throat was exposed.

'Idiot, you know that's not what I mean, although, come to think of it...' He leaned closer and licked her neck with little flicking movements of his tongue... 'Mmm, tastes good.'

Gemma laid down her pencil and closed her diary.

'Finished?' Sam asked. 'That was quick. I thought today's entry would have taken half the night.'

She smiled at him. A rich smile, full of love—sexy love, maternal love, tenderness.

'What was there to say?' She bent and kissed her son's cheek and raised her shining emerald green eyes to Sam. 'Except that today was a perfect ending to a perfect year? I wouldn't have changed it by one iota. You've loved and cherished Daisy and me, just as you promised. And to crown it all, you put the cherry...' She dimpled. 'No, two cherries on the cake. I feel the most blessed woman in the world.'

The church clock chimed a measured, sonorous twelve.

With a noisy slurp, Tara finished the last of her milk. Sam pulled hard at the bottle to release the teat from the rosebud mouth. It came away suddenly with a loud sucking plop.

Sam grinned and stared down at his small daughter. 'How do you do that with such a pretty little mouth—apply suction like a vacuum cleaner?' he asked.

Tara stared up at him with wide eyes, not quite blue, not quite green, and gave a satisfied burp and a beatific smile.

'I think that's all the answer you're going to get,' said Gemma with a soft chuckle.

Sam leaned across and kissed her. 'You know, dear heart, Tara's mouth is exactly like yours.'

Gemma looked down at her son. 'And Timothy's got your nose,' she said.

Sam laughed. 'Then honour is satisfied. They're a nice mixture of Fellows and Mallory.'

'I think Old Harry would call them a pigeon pair,' said Gemma.

Sam kissed her again. 'I like it,' he murmured. 'I can live with that.'

MEDICAL ROMANCE™

Large Print

Titles for the next six months…

September

THE GIRL NEXT DOOR	Caroline Anderson
DR BRIGHT'S EXPECTATIONS	Abigail Gordon
IDYLLIC INTERLUDE	Helen Shelton
AN ENTICING PROPOSAL	Meredith Webber

October

A FAMILY TO CARE FOR	Judy Campbell
POTENTIAL HUSBAND	Lucy Clark
TENDER LOVING CARE	Jennifer Taylor
ONCE A WISH	Carol Wood

November

DIAGNOSIS DEFERRED	Rebecca Lang
COURTING CATHIE	Helen Shelton
TRUST ME	Meredith Webber
TWICE A KISS	Carol Wood

MILLS & BOON®

Makes any time special™

MEDICAL ROMANCE™

Large Print

December

WINNING HER BACK	Lilian Darcy
FALLING FOR A STRANGER	Janet Ferguson
FOR PERSONAL REASONS	Leah Martyn
LOVE ME	Meredith Webber

January 2001

DOCTORS AT ODDS	Drusilla Douglas
HEART AT RISK	Helen Shelton
GREATER THAN RICHES	Jennifer Taylor
MARRY ME	Meredith Webber

February

NURSE FRIDAY	Margaret O'Neill
A MAN TO BE TRUSTED	Gill Sanderson
PRESCRIPTIONS AND PROMISES	Jessica Matthews
DANGER - DR HEARTBREAK	Elisabeth Scott

MILLS & BOON®

Makes any time special™